COURT
OF THE
DARK FAE

www.mascotbooks.com

Court of the Dark Fae

©2023 Aiysha Qureshi. All Rights Reserved. No part of this publication may be reproduced, stored in a retrieval system or transmitted in any form by any means electronic, mechanical, or photocopying, recording or otherwise without the permission of the author.

This is a work of fiction. Names, characters, businesses, places, events, and incidents are either the products of the author's imagination or used in a fictitious manner. Any resemblance to actual persons, living or dead, or actual events is purely coincidental.

For more information, please contact:
Mascot Books, an imprint of Amplify Publishing Group
620 Herndon Parkway, Suite 220
Herndon, VA 20170
info@mascotbooks.com

Library of Congress Control Number: 2023907677

CPSIA Code: PRV0623A
ISBN-13: 978-1-63755-627-6

Printed in the United States

For my friends and family who believed in me. With special thanks to my friend, Ashlyn, for being my biggest supporter.

COURT
⬦ OF THE
DARK FAE

Aiysha Qureshi

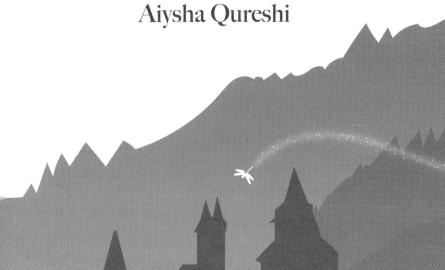

PROLOGUE

Hidden from the eyes of mortals was a land home to many fantastical creatures, all who seemingly lived together peacefully. This place, governed by magic and those who wielded it, was known as the realm of Moira.

The laws of magic ruled that the most just individuals would be crowned as the high rulers, a responsibility that was not to be taken lightly. The only way to remove the title of high ruler was for the individual to be defeated in a battle, something that had not been done for centuries.

To the north was the court of the Dark Fae, ruled by High King Oren and his wife, High Queen Nerida. True to their titles, they were just and kind, and they took care of the other courts in their times of need.

To the south was the court of the Light Fae, ruled by King Faven. He was jealous Oren had been named high king. Already, Oren was the most powerful ruler in the realm, and to top it off, now he ruled it all.

The upper eastern lands were home to the Moon Elves, ruled by Prince Lyndell, a close friend of the high king. Though often clumsy and annoying, the prince had a good heart, and whether Oren admitted it or not, he was one of the few individuals whom he fully trusted with his life.

The lower eastern lands were ruled by Prince Sol. The Sun Elves, cousins of the Moon Elves, were a spiteful and prideful bunch, always playing cruel tricks to show off their cleverness. They had once caused Prince Lyndell's hair color to change during an important meeting, thus tensions between the two kingdoms ran high.

The western lands housed the Dwarves, ruled by Queen Nessa. She had no tolerance for anyone and was the cruelest creature that dwelled in the realm. She too was jealous of Oren's position as the high king and sought to become the high ruler herself.

The Trolls lived in mountainous cave systems that were scattered throughout the realm, so in essence, not really living in one section over the other. They were ruled by King Thistle and Queen Nettle.

The Goblins, having no interest in the doings of the other creatures in the realm, lived in a moated castle that had long been abandoned and was now a heavily guarded fortress ruled by the Goblin king, Nash.

The Gnomes lived in the forests, ruled by their stoic and composed leader, Lord Obsidian. Within the trees lived the pixies and their queen, Amaryllis. Together they lived and protected one another in peace and harmony.

The Shapeshifters and Dragons lived together in the mountains, each ruling their own section—Queen Callista ruled the bottoms of the mountains, while Lord Alaric ruled the tops.

In time, the two would combine their kingdoms, for Queen Callista had fallen for the Dragon lord.

The Unicorns lived among the clouds, ruled by their leader, Lord Silverlight. Rarely did they come down to the ground to involve themselves with the rest of the realm unless it was to speak to Oren.

This year, the harvest moon was on full display amongst the twinkling stars, and as the rulers of each court gathered around and ate to their hearts' content, no one knew of the growing animosity that Queen Nessa and King Faven had towards the high king and queen.

And no one would come to know just how deep that hatred would become until many years later, when the body of one of Oren's dear friends was found, lying in a pool of blood in the human realm.

CHAPTER 1

"Just southwest of the Valley of Kings lies the Valley of Queens. As the name suggests, it was mostly reserved for the wives of the pharaohs."

The professor's monotonous voice had been droning on for almost an hour.

Though history was Willow's favorite topic, her professor's voice did nothing to interest the class that currently sat in front of him. Time seemed to crawl by as the hands on the clock moved so slowly. Most of the students opted to aimlessly scroll on their phones; some posting on their social media accounts about the various winter vacations they would soon be on.

"Students, I expect a ten-page essay on the Valley of Kings when you return. There are no extensions or exceptions to the due date on this essay, unless you fail to show up to class due to your untimely demise. You may all go now," he finished abruptly.

As soon as the professor dismissed them, many of the students rushed past Willow in a great hurry.

One student with green-streaked black hair and amber-colored eyes approached Willow's desk and shoved her books and notes to the ground.

"Still taking notes like a good little student, Blackplum?"

Willow rolled her eyes. Kalen Isley, the neighborhood brat who had unfortunately followed her into college, had been a thorn in her side for as long as she could remember.

"Can't you come up with a better line, Isley? You've been saying that since the first grade."

"At least I didn't have to get a scholarship from the school to afford going here. How pathetic do you feel knowing that the school practically paid you to come here just because you can write!" he finished with a laugh, smirking at Willow as he left the room.

Sighing in defeat, she bent down to pick up her things. She slung her pink messenger bag over one shoulder and stuffed the papers inside. As she made her way out of the classroom, her gaze flickered over to the white analog clock on the wall. It was 3:00 p.m.

No time like the present to finish her essay.

Willow pushed open the wooden oak doors to the library.

The smell was a strange yet comforting mix of herbal tea and new and old books. She felt the tension in her body release a bit. People were gathered around tables with books, writing utensils, and papers scattered throughout. The familiar shelves were filled to the brim with books. Without glancing at the signs, she made her way to the shelves dedicated to modern and ancient world history. There were several options for ancient Egyptian history. After taking a few seconds to scan them, Willow grabbed the one that seemed the most comprehensive.

Satisfied with her find, she found a quiet corner and sat in a comfortable armchair, the massive book propped on her lap, and soon she was pulled into a world of pharaohs and pyramids.

Before she knew it, night had fallen and she could see the moon had risen from a nearby window. To her surprise, the clock read 8:00 p.m., which was closing time for the library. She stood up and threw her books and papers into her messenger bag. As she pushed open the wooden doors, her face was greeted by a blast of cold air and the bright light of the moon.

It was a beautiful winter night. The moon was out, and stars littered the sky like a thousand tiny diamonds. A slight breeze was blowing, but her dusty-rose-colored sweater and black jeans were warm enough. The low heels of her boots clacked against the sidewalk as she walked home.

The only thing she really looked forward to was the frozen pizza sitting alone in the freezer in her equally lonely apartment.

Suddenly a shadow fell over her, but just as quickly as it had appeared, it vanished, falling into the bushes that were to the side of the sidewalk; just beyond them was a thick forest.

Her curiosity piqued, Willow pushed past the bushes and stepped into the trees, and what she saw defied any rational explanation she could come up with.

A figure was lying motionless on the forest floor. It looked like a man, or at least part man. Pale skin glinted in the moonlight. His ink-black hair covered one side of his face. Willow blinked several times, pushing the darkness away and allowing her eyes to adjust.

Looking down, she saw black, butterfly-like wings with white spots that sparkled like rainbow-colored gems jutting out from his back.

This is impossible, Willow thought, blinking furiously and rubbing her eyes. He looked like a fairy, but fairies were small and mischievous creatures, at least according to the books she had read.

The figure in front of her was significantly larger in size.

A silver crown with a purple jeweled dragonfly sat on his head. He was dressed in a gray tunic embroidered with blue leaves and pants colored a smokey gray, tucked into tall, gray boots. His regal ensemble was accentuated with several sparkly piercings along his ears. Completing this dazzling display, the fairy had a silver necklace with a pendant in the shape of a dragonfly.

Willow's stomach turned when her eyes drifted to his midsection.

Blood as black as ink oozed from a wound, staining the ground beneath him.

Despite her shock, she dug through her messenger bag, hoping that she had something to stanch the bleeding and dress the fairy's wound. The first thing she grabbed was her jacket, which she quickly pressed to his side to stop the blood. As soon as her jacket touched his wound, a soft pink glow coming from beneath it blinded her for a moment, and the bleeding stopped soon after.

Willow yanked her hands back, not knowing how the fairy had healed himself while he was unconscious. Shaking her head, she saw that the wound was still raw, so she took out the first aid kit that she usually carried. After she had found herself in a situation where she had needed the same supplies, although not to the extent of the person lying on the ground, she had thought it was best to be prepared.

As gently as she could, she began to clean the area of the fairy's wound with a bit of antiseptic, when suddenly, a pale hand reached out and grabbed her wrist. Two piercing blue eyes bore into her—but each eye was different. The left eye was sapphire, and the right eye was the color of the ocean. The fairy jolted up, and the ocean-colored eye was quickly hidden behind his hair.

"Who are you, and what do you think you're doing?" asked the cultured voice attached to the man with the mismatched blue eyes.

"I'm trying to clean and dress your wound, so you don't bleed to death, obviously," she said, her voice laced with sarcasm.

"I bet you think you're so clever. You think that you can injure the high king of the Dark Fae Court and then pretend to dress his wound?" he asked with equal if not greater sarcasm.

Willow rolled her eyes; he obviously had the wrong impression of her. She had no idea of what he was talking about, either.

"Well? Answer me! Or are you just going to sit there and pretend that you're not involved in any plots that end with my death?"

She could hear the mistrust and anger in his tone, eyes widening at the fact that he thought she was trying to off him.

"I found you like this. You were hurt, and I didn't want you to bleed to death, so I cleaned and tried to dress your wound. I think you may have gotten stabbed."

She answered as calmly as she could, hoping he might see that she was indeed trying to help him. He stared at her with his sapphire eye for what seemed like the longest moment and then regained his composure, releasing a long sigh.

"I deeply apologize for my rudeness, but for a stranger, a human nonetheless, to attempt to heal a Fae—who in your world is technically not supposed to exist—is quite uncommon. Humans are known to be selfish creatures who only seek to gain the favor of fairies and, in rare cases, the Fae courts. Because of this, we have elected not to communicate with this realm often," he explained this with a slightly bitter tone, though it was more polite than his original outburst.

"You don't have to believe me, but I don't expect anything from you. I didn't take care of your wound because I want something in return," she said.

He looked at her, his brow creasing. "No one is that kind. Do you expect me to believe a human saved me without a thought to their own selfish motives? Perhaps you saved me in hopes of gaining some favor. Humans are so easily misled by their desires."

"You can believe what you wish. I certainly can't change your mind." She didn't need the favor of some alluring, smug, and egotistical king.

"Well now, my dear, you certainly are brave speaking to a Fae king with such boldness. No one speaks that way to me in my kingdom. I find it to be quite amusing," he finished with a chuckle, the mirth evident in his visible eye.

Willow silently scoffed at his behavior; mere moments ago he was visibly angry, and that anger had somehow turned to amusement.

"Might I ask your name, my dear?" he asked with a smirk on his face.

"I don't know. You haven't exactly told me your name."

"Very well. If you will tell me your name, then I shall tell you mine," he replied.

She rolled her eyes again; he must have thought he was so full of glittering wit and charm. Then she responded. "My name is Willow Blackplum."

"Charmed to meet you, Miss Blackplum. My name is High King Oren of the Dark Fae Court," he responded with a smile.

"Well, your majesty, I hate to interrupt our lovely introductions, but I need to finish wrapping your wound. I can't risk you getting an infection from an open wound."

"Perhaps you could assist me in standing up, I may have a better chance at recovering in my court," he said while wincing slightly.

"I'll help you get back home. But I'm not exactly sure how you're going to go about doing that. You might accidentally injure yourself again or reopen your wound."

A small laugh escaped from his mouth. "I wouldn't dream of injuring myself twice, my dear. There is a specific place in this forest that I may need your assistance in getting to. Do you humans have experience in opening portals to different worlds?"

"Most humans don't know how to use magic, so I would say no," she replied.

He sighed. "Such a pity. I guess I have no choice but to open the portal myself."

"Alright, your majesty, let's get you home then," Willow responded, rolling her eyes and helping the Fae to stand upright.

She let him lean on her a bit, since he couldn't put his full weight on his own legs without aggravating his wound.

While Willow and the Dark Fae king walked in a surprisingly comfortable silence, she couldn't help but let a question escape from her lips.

"How exactly would I help transport you back to your court? I don't have any experience with magic."

"You don't really need any experience to help me. And although you say that you don't have any experience with magic, I can sense traces of magical energy within you. I am most certain of this. No other individual in the nearby area is exuding the amount of energy that you are," he responded.

"That's not possible, I never even thought that Fae existed. How could I have powers or any magic?" she asked.

The night kept on getting stranger. First, she had run into a ruler of a realm, and now he was telling her that she had magic?

"It's possible you may be a Faeling. An individual who has a Fae and a human for parents, though their existence is very rare and their magic is highly sought after. However, it can only be channeled using a wand or a spell book. Although your magic . . . it feels different. It's much stronger and wilder, more so than that of a normal Faeling."

He answered, interrupting the many thoughts that had begun to swirl around in her mind. How was this even happening?

She had always thought that she was just an ordinary person. The only story she had read regarding Fae in the human realm was Shakespeare's play, *A Midsummer Night's Dream*. This completely threw off her entire understanding of the universe.

"Well, I guess we can figure that out later. How exactly are we going to be able to find the place that will allow you to go home?" she asked, snapping herself out of her thought spiral.

She was shaken by the revelation that she was something other than what she had always thought of herself as. She didn't want to think about the different possibilities that were running through her mind.

"There is a gateway between realms in the forest. The residual magic stored in my necklace is like a bridge, connecting that gateway to the magic inside," he said as he spun his dragonfly pendant in his hand. "So, in essence, the portal reacts with my pendant. When I am close by, it starts to glow," he explained, quelling her curiosity.

"That seems straightforward . . . and very dangerous. What if someone takes your necklace while you're hurt or unconscious and gains access to your kingdom?" she asked.

She felt like the Dark Fae king was endangering his kingdom with such an easy-to-steal object as the necklace.

He chuckled.

"My kingdom, or my court as it is formally called, doesn't just appear to anyone should they manage to have my pendant in their possession. That is only part of my magical flair. For the spell to work, there must be an item upon which it is cast. In this case, the item I chose to cast the spell on is my pendant."

Staring at a loose thread at the cuff of her sleeve, she looked thoughtful for a moment before responding.

"That's a relief. I thought anyone would be able to get into your court if they got their hands on your necklace."

"I hope you weren't planning on stealing it, Miss Blackplum." he said, the trace of a smirk evident on his face.

"You wound me, your majesty. I would never steal your necklace."

The Dark Fae king chuckled at her response. "Perhaps not."

After that exchange, they continued walking until they came upon a small frozen-over creek, which oddly enough was surrounded by an arch of blooming trees.

"What were you doing outside of your court, anyway?"

He looked away in embarrassment before responding hesitantly. "If you must know, I was searching for a gift to give to my daughter. Fae live long lives, so not many things fascinate us the way they do in the human realm."

"What's the reason you didn't take any form of protection or guards with you?" she asked.

"I am the high king of the Dark Fae Court; I don't need protection from anyone."

She scoffed at that.

"Do you know how you got injured?" Willow asked.

"Contrary to your apparent belief, Ms. Blackplum, I do, in fact, know how I got injured. You were correct in guessing that I had gotten stabbed. I was unable to see who it was; they attacked me far too quickly and with a sword," he shared quietly.

She shook her head.

"And that is why you shouldn't have gone alone. I also didn't think the high and mighty Dark Fae king had a daughter."

He laughed in response.

"Of course, I have a daughter. Her name is Wisp. She and her mother are very important to me."

"I think she takes after me, though she's quite shy, but she has her mother's kindness."

"Let's hope she's not as charming as you," Willow joked.

"Oh, I suppose you think you're amusing, don't you Miss Blackplum?" he chuckled.

"I don't think I'm amusing; I know I am."

He turned his head to give her an unamused stare.

She couldn't help but fall into banter with him as if she had known him for years instead of just a few minutes. He interrupted their bantering with a few questions of his own.

"What of your family, Miss Blackplum? Surely, they must be worried about you, having been gone for so many hours."

Willow was caught a bit off guard at his question and concern. Then she visibly sighed.

Willow's family wasn't a topic that she liked to discuss with anyone for a number of reasons. Yet the Dark Fae king's presence had an air of understanding and calmness that she felt comfortable answering his questions.

"I honestly don't believe that they would care even if they knew."

"Oh?" He was surprised by her response.

She could tell his curiosity was now piqued, so she decided to continue.

"Truthfully, I haven't spoken to my family in years. My sister didn't like me. Most likely she still doesn't. She hated me so much that she told my mother and father rumors about me that weren't true. Not only that, but she would blame me for things that were not in my control, and my family still took her side."

Willow paused and looked at the ground, trying not to let emotions overwhelm her.

"One thing led to another, and pretty soon my parents and I were always arguing. It was mostly my father who would take the metaphorical knife and twist it. It got to a point where they told me that it would have been better if I had just left and never came back. I took whatever I could carry, walked out, and never looked back."

The Dark Fae king was silent for a moment.

"I don't think anyone deserves that, let alone you, my dear," he said with kind eyes.

"I also think what you did was very wise. Rather than letting the conflict consume your life, you decided to leave it all behind and focus on your life."

Willow sighed wistfully, as they continued to walk deeper into the forest. "It was wise, alright. Now they act as if they only have one daughter. I miss what I once had, but the rumors and lies made it hard to live with any of them."

"Have you ever tried to explain how manipulative your sister is? Perhaps they didn't mean for things to happen the way they did," suggested the Dark Fae.

Willow shook her head.

"Believe me, I've tried several times after I left to clear the air between us. They aren't willing to listen to anything I have to say. And I have no intention of asking them to forgive me for things I clearly didn't do."

Willow hadn't really thought about her family in all the years since she had left. Honestly, there really wasn't much to think about; they chose their path, and she chose hers.

"They definitely don't sound like they are worth talking to, especially since they don't care about you enough to ignore the idiotic things that come out of your sister's mouth."

He then scoffed, seemingly at his continuing thoughts.

Then changing the subject, he pointed ahead of them.

"Do you see the arch of blooming trees? All I must do is walk up to the entrance, hold up my pendant, and of course cast my spell so that I may go to my court."

"I think you explained it before your majesty," she teased, a trace of a smile returning to her face.

"You wound me my dear. I didn't mention the arch of trees before, only the spell."

He answered back with an equal amount of teasing in his tone.

While he stood in front of the arch, he held his pendant up and began casting his spell, purple sparks flying from his fingertips and the scent of violets filled the air.

As the door to his realm opened, there was a sudden rush of wind. The blossoms blew off the trees and began swirling around, flowing through the arch, filling in the empty space. The wall of blossoms became transparent, and his stunning kingdom came into view.

Willow felt a pang of sadness. She knew this was where they had to say goodbye. They had just met, but she felt like she had found a friend in the king.

As if sensing her thoughts, the Dark Fae king turned to her. "Would you like to see my court?"

Briefly thinking about the empty apartment she had to go back to, she decided to take the Fae king up on his offer.

"I would love to see it!"

He smiled at her response, and the two of them stepped in through the portal.

As their bodies passed through, particles of glowing energy engulfed them. Willow felt a warm sensation as they crossed from mundane to magical. She felt strangely comforted once she emerged in the unfamiliar realm.

She saw lush green hills, flowering trees, a sky so blue, the golden sun shining down, and millions of flowers, butterflies, and dragonflies all over the place. Oren's castle was gray, surrounded by a contrast of colorful flowers.

"Welcome to the realm of Moira, specifically the northern part where my court lies. I do hope that you are quite impressed by the view, Miss Blackplum. After all, no human has ever set foot here," he said with a smug look.

She rolled her eyes. "I suppose you think you're so charming."

"Thank you for admitting that, my dear."

Her cheeks colored slightly at that, but before she could come up with a retort, a loud crashing sound came from the front gates of Oren's castle. Despite being injured, he reached into his tall boots and pulled out what appeared to be fancy switchblades.

"Stay behind me, Willow," he said firmly, all traces of teasing disappeared, leaving no room for any arguments. A figure fell out in front of Oren, and his expression changed from worry to utter annoyance.

The individual who had fallen in front of them had long red flaming locks that fell past his shoulders. His eyes were the color of raw emeralds, and he had pointed ears. His skin was as silvery as the moon itself, and he wore what appeared to be a silver tunic, adorned with red crescent moons and matching pants, completed with tall black boots. On his head was a silver crown of moons, each in a different phase, finished with a red jeweled rabbit resting in the center. On his neck hung a silver pendant in the shape of a rabbit; its eyes were ruby gems.

As he picked himself up from the ground, he let one statement after the other spill out from his mouth. "Wow! A real human in the Fae realm! Oren must be losing his mind to let you come here! Why did he let you come here? Are you in trouble? Did you insult him by accident like I did one time?"

As soon as those words had left his mouth, his head was met with a smack from the Dark Fae king himself.

"Lyndell. Have you no filter on that large mouth of yours?" Oren asked him in annoyance.

"Ow! I was just surprised. You don't have to be so mean, you know," grumbled the red-haired individual as he rubbed his head.

"Well, who told you could come here and make so much noise?" Oren asked.

"Nerida said I could come over and play with Wisp!" he whined.

"Idiot," Oren muttered before taking a deep breath.

"What's your name?" the redhead asked Willow cheerfully,

ignoring the fact that his friend called him an idiot and that he probably scared him to death.

"My name is Willow. It's nice to meet you."

"Hi, Willow! I'm Prince Lyndell of the Moon Elf Court! And best friend to High Dark Fae King Oren, unfortunately."

"Will you stop your incessant chattering, you flaming matchstick? It's giving me quite the headache," the Fae king stated in irritation.

"You're so mean! I was only trying to be friendly to her. Why are you in such a sour mood?" asked the oblivious Moon Elf.

"Two very obvious reasons. One, he's injured and needs medical attention. Two, you decided to make a noise, and he's annoyed because he probably thought you were an intruder."

Willow thought it would be best if she tried to quell the situation before Oren's friend made him angrier than he already was.

"Wait, you're injured?" How did you get injured? Did the human hurt you?" He squinted in suspicion at Willow.

"Don't be an idiot. I'm fine, I just need to properly clean my wound and change my bandages. Which I can't do if I'm standing here talking to you. Miss Blackplum was just about to help me get inside so if you can move, Red, that would be great." The irritation was ever growing in Oren's tone, but his friend was too oblivious to hear it.

"My name's not Red! It's Lyndell! You don't usually carry medical supplies with you. Where did you even get those?"

Before the lovely gentlemen could continue with their equally lovely conversation, she decided to interrupt. "I would love to hear two grown rulers argue like children all day, but we really need to get you inside, your majesty. You know, before the wound reopens and you start bleeding . . . again."

"Well said, my dear. The sooner I can fix my wound the better," the Dark Fae king responded.

"I'll get my answer from you sooner or later!" Lyndell declared with a determined look on his face. The Dark Fae king shoved his friend and walked past him.

"Hey!"

Ignoring Lyndell, they made their way up the steps of the castle. King Oren was greeted by someone at the entrance. Willow assumed this person was his queen because she was wearing a crown and because of her air of nobility. Long, caramel-colored locks fell in layers to her back, and her eyes were a warm brown color. She had on a red-and-black gothic-style dress with layers, embroidered with silver vines all over, finished with ruby red slippers adorned with black lace. On her head, she wore a crown of red and black roses. She had red wings reminiscent of a butterfly that were tipped with elegant black designs around the edges.

She gasped as soon as she saw them. "Oren! Darling, you're hurt! Are you alright?"

"Hello, Butterfly. Worry not my darling queen, I am fine. Had it not been for Miss Blackplum here, I would not have been able to make my way home," he finished, as he kissed her hand.

She blushed and turned to Willow. "Oh, thank you so much! I was so worried about Oren. He always gets into trouble whenever he goes out."

"You're welcome, your majesty. He wasn't injured too badly; I didn't do that much. But I can only imagine the trouble he gives you," Willow responded with a small laugh.

"Oh, you're so sweet! You can call me Nerida! Anyone who cares enough to stop and help my king is welcome here. And tell me about it, he thinks he's invincible," she finished with a laugh of her own.

"I'm still here, in case the both of you forgot."

"Well, you are getting heavy, Fae king," Willow retorted.

"I am not heavy, Miss Blackplum."

"Of course not, dear. Let's take you to the infirmary," said the queen.

At the infirmary, Nerida cleaned his wound. She poured a strange pink liquid on his wound that smelled like berries and flowers. Oren's wound began to close, as if there were invisible stitches sealing it shut. It looked as if he hadn't gotten injured in the first place.

"That feels much better," the Dark Fae king said, and before he could say anything else, a red blur pushed past the doors and barreled into the room.

"Alright, you're healed now. Tell me what happened, how did you get hurt so badly? Who hurt you?" demanded the Moon Elf prince.

Oren sighed in annoyance and ignored Lyndell's questions. Lyndell huffed. "Fine. Don't tell me then! I'll just ask Willow when you leave."

His statement was met with a smack on the back of his head by his friend.

"Ow! Why do you keep doing that to me, Oren? Do I look like I need to be smacked by you all the time?"

"Yes, in fact you do. Who says that I must tell you what happened? And don't even think about asking Miss Blackplum. She doesn't have to sit and listen to your endless inquiries about how and where and even why I got injured."

"Alright fine. No need to be so hostile. I won't pry, but I'll be back later," answered the Moon Elf prince sheepishly while he slowly walked out of the infirmary, seemingly tripping on nothing as a loud crash was heard followed by a thud and then a shout. "I'm okay!" the prince shouted as he left.

Oren sighed in annoyance, but before he could say anything, Nerida interrupted. "Oren darling, you should get some rest. You were out all night, and even though your wound has healed, it's best you get some sleep," she finished sweetly.

Oren's annoyed expression softened before he responded to his queen. "No need to worry about me, Nerida. I am fine thanks to you and Miss Blackplum."

"Stubborn Fae," Willow muttered

"You really need to speak up, my dear, otherwise I might think you're talking about me."

"Don't make me force you to rest, your highness."

"You know, you can call me Oren, and I'd like to see you try. You would have to catch me first," he answered cheekily.

Willow rolled her eyes. "You really know how to talk your way out of anything, don't you?"

"Dearest Willow, I would never dream of it. But since you keep admitting I'm charming, who am I to stop you?"

"I'm going to pretend you didn't say that." She resisted the urge to roll her eyes, this time at least.

"Oren, if you don't rest, then I won't let you attend court meetings," his queen interjected sweetly with a mischievous smile.

"Come now, my dear Nerida, surely you wouldn't do that to me."

"I wouldn't, if you rested."

"I think she's serious. I'd listen to her if I were you, your highness." Willow chuckled at the fate of the Dark Fae king.

"You two think this is funny, don't you? Teaming up on a defenseless Fae king."

"I seem to recall you saying that you have some charm. So, talk your way out of this one, oh charming one," Willow couldn't help but saying, though if she was being honest, maybe she did think he was charming.

"You and Nerida must think you are a real dream team."

"You're only saying that because you don't have any arguments for that Fae king," Willow finished, looking smug for once, as opposed to Oren who looked like he'd been defeated.

CRASH!

While they were having fun at Oren's expense, the windows suddenly shattered, and shards of glass went flying everywhere.

Had Oren not swiftly put up a magical shield, the glass would most likely have pierced their bodies. In the midst of it all stood a fairy decked out in golden armor. The only thing missing from his armor was a helmet; it was as though he wanted to be identified. A curtain of golden hair fell past his shoulders. Fiery orange eyes stared at everyone in the room; their irises filled with an intense malice and hatred. His wings were moth-like. In his right hand, he gripped a golden sword whose hilt was decorated with golden suns and outlined with orange topaz.

"Such a shame that you still live, Oren. That wound should have killed you right away," the dark and venomous voice thundered.

"I always knew the Light Fae were despicable, but going after me? That's a new low, even for you. I knew very well that I wasn't liked by everyone in the realm, yet none of them have tried to end my life in the way that the Light Alliance has," Oren said.

"At least I have some class. I don't proceed to bring filthy humans into my court. I knew you were an incapable high king, but even I know that humans aren't allowed here."

"That is the most ridiculous statement that has ever come out of your mouth, Heliodor! You know as well as I do that ludicrous rule does not and has not existed for centuries. Even so, you coming here has nothing to do with that. You're only here to finish the job you barely started!" The blindingly bright figure lifted his sword and lunged at the closest person he could attack, which turned out to be Nerida. Not thinking at all, Willow threw herself between the Dark Fae queen and the oncoming attacker.

Closing her eyes, she waited for the blow. But nothing happened. She opened her eyes and much to her shock, silver sparks were flying out of her fingertips and binding themselves around the gold figure, as if they were actual ropes. Suddenly, it felt as if she was channeling all her fear and uncertainty into the binding energy coming out of her hands.

"What is the meaning of this? How dare you stop me! Do you know who I am?"

"Shut your mouth, Heliodor! How dare you try and attack the high queen!" seethed Oren, grabbing the Light Fae by the front of his armor.

"Let me out of these binds and I'll show you how a real king rules a realm! You can't even protect your family against me! I'll kill you and this filthy pest along with the rest of your family!"

SMACK!

Nerida, having heard enough garbage coming out of Heliodor's mouth, slapped him, leaving a strange burn in the shape of a handprint. "That's quite enough! I will not tolerate any more of your disrespect, especially toward an individual who does not even know you. Willow defended me from your attack and could have gotten seriously injured herself!" She paused for a moment. "Lady Anthea!" Nerida was furious to the point of calling out for someone to deal with Heliodor.

A Dark Fae knight with long flowing purple hair fluttered into the room as soon as she was called. This Fae was dressed in silver armor and tall black boots and carried a black sword with blossoms engraved on its hilt and tiny pink gemstones scattered across. Long silver earrings with pink sapphires dangled from her ears, glinting in the light. What drew Willow's eyes to her appearance the most were the purple and white butterfly wings protruding from her back.

"Please take this villainous Light Fae to the dungeons. And don't worry about his binds. I have a feeling that they won't disappear anytime soon," Nerida ordered.

"As you wish, my queen," Lady Anthea replied as she hauled the Light Fae to his feet and forcefully shoved him toward a hallway.

"You're all doomed to die! I will see to it personally that the Dark Fae Court is wiped out by my army! Then you will all have the pleasure of bowing to me before I end your pathetic lives!" Heliodor swore this as he was being dragged out of the room.

"Shut up, you imbecile! You're incredibly lucky my king didn't end your life!" Lady Anthea stated to the struggling Light Fae.

As they left the room, Oren and Nerida were conversing with one another. Willow's eyes felt heavy, and she found herself unable to keep them open. Soon after, darkness welcomed her into its embrace.

Oren rushed to catch Willow before she hit the ground, looking over her in concern.

"The sudden rush of using her powers must have been too much for her. I don't think she was expecting that," said Oren.

"Do you think she's a Faeling?" the Dark Fae queen pondered.

"It's a possibility. I did sense magic within her when we first met, although it is a bit different from Faeling magic," Oren shared.

"Whatever the case may be, she needs to rest. She did a brave thing, saving my life not knowing what would happen to hers," Nerida said with concern lacing her voice.

"Indeed. Let me carry her to a guest room; you should go and see if Wisp is still asleep. I've no doubt that the noise must have awoken her by now."

Oren gently picked Willow up from the ground and carried her to the dragonfly wing of the castle. The halls were decked with metal carvings of dragonflies, banners in silver and purple hung from the ceiling, a trail of dragonflies adorning each one. The room he had taken her to was mostly gray with hints of silver that made the gray color stand out even more. Everything from the walls to the bed were engraved with black silhouettes of dragon-flies that danced around animatedly. A large wardrobe filled with clothing stood in the corner, and opposite to that was a vanity laden with brushes, combs, accessories, and various cosmetics.

The Fae king laid Willow on the bed and pulled the blanket over her unconscious form. "Watch over her," he ordered the dragonflies.

"Yes, of course, your majesty!" chirped the dragonflies.

As he left, the Fae king closed the door behind him and made his way into the throne room.

Along the way, he caught up with Nerida.

"Is Wisp still asleep?" Oren asked.

"Thankfully, she is. At least all the noise didn't wake her. What about Willow?"

"She will recover. She just needs to rest; it was a shock to her body, using powers that she didn't know existed. But I would like to know how in the realm Heliodor managed to get into my castle, especially with the protective barrier I've placed! There are a select few people allowed within this castle, and I want to know who let that menace in here!" he seethed.

"It's very possible that someone in the royal guard let him through the barrier. They are the only ones besides Lyndell who have permission to come and go from the castle," Nerida suggested.

"That does not narrow down the traitor by much. It could be any one of them. Many of the guards have reasons to betray me." Oren scowled at the floor in thought.

"You might be right about that. I think you should meet with your court and allies in the morning. I have a feeling that war may not be avoidable this time," Nerida advised.

Deep down in Oren's dungeon, Heliodor was slumped against the stone wall of his cell, the silver binds still tightly wrapped around him. A hooded figure appeared in front of him and snapped their fingers, then the bonds disappeared from around the Light Fae's body.

"It's about time you showed up! Do you have any idea how humiliating it is to be beaten by a nobody?"

"You're a fool, Heliodor!" hissed a cold, calculated voice. "How could you not sense it? Oren just brought over the key to the demise of the Light Alliance. Possibly the last known Faeling in existence."

"That's preposterous! Faelings don't exist; they died out centuries ago!" Heliodor snapped.

"Apparently, you're not powerful enough to sense raw magic given that you let someone with less magic than yourself defeat you," seethed the cool voice.

"I don't need you to ridicule me. I'm not the one betraying the Dark Fae," Heliodor replied smugly.

"Shut your mouth, half-wit. I'm pulling all the strings here. If I didn't have to attend court in the morning then I wouldn't stay here and release you. I'm going to create the illusion that you are still here. It should last for a while. Leave when the last guards leave for court, by then I'll have an illusion of you still in this cell."

With that said, the hooded figure melted into the shadows, leaving behind the illusion of a still-bound Heliodor and a silver-and-purple-jeweled key in the hands of the imprisoned Light Fae.

CHAPTER 2

A loud crash reverberated throughout the castle, instantly alerting the Dark Fae king who had but a few hours of sleep. He threw the doors to his throne room open, silver and black switchblades gripped tightly between his fingers.

Much to his everlasting annoyance, a red-haired figure was sprawled on the ground amongst large pieces of a giant gray crystal vase that was once whole. Oren crossed his arms and stared at Lyndell with his most unimpressed expression.

"Give me one really good reason I shouldn't throw you down the steps right this moment."

"Because I'm your favorite friend?" Lyndell suggested.

Oren glared at him. "You're not my *only* friend."

"Well, you're lucky I showed up for court to begin with! It's way too early to be awake!" Lyndell squeaked.

"Is that the best reason you can come up with?"

"What's going on?" Nerida questioned as she entered the hallway, glancing at the large shards of the broken vase.

"Oh, hello Nerida! I might have tripped and accidentally broken a vase."

"I was just about to throw him out for that."

"You are both acting like children. It's just a vase, Oren." Nerida was not amused in the slightest at their antics.

"Oren started yelling at me first."

"Shut your mouth, you idiot."

"You're not being very nice!"

"You were nice to Willow, though! Where is she anyway?"

"She doesn't annoy me the way you do, and I don't have to tell you anything."

"What do you mean I annoy you? And why won't you tell me?"

"Isn't that obvious? I don't have to tell you everything, you overripe tomato."

"This really isn't the time to be arguing. We need to see if Willow is awake, and then we have must convene in the West Hall for the meeting with our allies," Nerida interrupted, exasperated.

"Perhaps we should bring her to the meeting with us, she was a witness when Heliodor attacked. Having her there would make our claims more credible. It would also be the best idea to keep her safe," the Dark Fae king unexpectedly said, forgetting his momentary ire at Lyndell.

"Are you sure that's a good idea? We don't have any idea how our allies will react to that," Nerida said, her thoughts wandering, not wanting the young woman to go through the trouble of appearing in a court full of creatures she didn't know.

"I don't doubt that our allies will react, but she's not safe by herself when we'll all be at the meeting. Someone in this castle likely knows. How else would that Light Fae be able to come in and try to attack us? I won't let anything happen to her, Nerida; she's not going to have to prove anything to anyone. She only needs to say that she was there when Heliodor attacked, otherwise it will seem as though we are just eager to cause trouble."

"It's not you I'm worried about. It's our allies. Not everyone is always on the same page and not everyone is welcoming," the Dark Fae queen stated with a hint of worry evident in her tone.

"Mom?" A small figure with long ink-black hair that fell past her shoulders walked sleepily into the throne room. Her eyes were two different colors—one a sapphire blue and the other a warm brown. Her dress was a pale blue, adorned with green leaves and pale pink flowers, navy blue slippers adorning her feet. Jutting out from her back were a pair of red and black butterfly-like wings with blue spots that sparkled like sapphires. "I heard everyone talking loudly, and it woke me up."

"Oops. I guess we were a little too loud." Lyndell said, laughing nervously.

"*We?* You are the one who tripped and broke a vase! If anything, that probably woke her up first!" Oren protested at the audacity of his friend.

"I said I was sorry!" Lyndell exclaimed with equal protest.

"Sorry doesn't help now, moron."

"Oren! Watch that language around Wisp! And Lyndell, go and see if any of our allies have arrived for the meeting."

"Alright, Nerida," responded the Elf prince, leaving the room.

He stuck his tongue out at the Fae king.

"Idiot," he muttered under his breath, much to the chagrin of

Nerida, who was currently gracing him with her most unamused stare.

"If you're done, I want you to brush Wisp's hair while I see if Willow is awake and able to attend the meeting."

"I thought I was going to see if Willow was awake," Oren whined.

"Oh no, you, are going to help your daughter with her hair. I'll be checking on Willow." She walked away leaving a bewildered Fae king with Wisp.

"Dad, is Mom angry with you?"

"No, she's not angry with me, Wisp."

"She usually helps me with my hair though. She only makes you do it when she's upset with you."

Oren hid an amused chuckle at that. "Who told you that? Come here, you little flower petal!"

He chased his daughter, who laughed in delight as they finally reached her pale blue and pink bedroom. Reaching for the hairbrush on her vanity, Oren deftly brushed Wisp's hair and tied it together with a pale blue ribbon.

"Mom does a better job."

"Does she now? I think I did a much better job this time," he finished with a small smile.

"What? Let me see. Wow! You put blue and pink roses in my hair, thank you!"

"You are welcome, Wisp. Come, let's go and wait outside the Northern Hall for your mother and our friend to come."

"What friend?"

"You'll see when your mother brings her."

They walked along the corridor until they came to a set of dark wooden doors emblazoned with a crest of a dragonfly; the handles of the doors were decorated with silver butterflies. Restless shouts and noises could be heard from the inside, and a familiar voice could be heard trying to calm them down.

"Everybody, please calm down!" a yell came from Lyndell.

"Where's the high king?"

"Who left you in charge?" Oren rolled his eyes; his allies were an impatient bunch, and Lyndell was an incompetent idiot.

"Honestly, why do I have to do everything myself?" Oren muttered.

"Dad, is Lyndell making your head hurt again?" Wisp asked.

"Yes dear, he is. Don't worry though, I want you to go and play. I'll send some guards over to keep an eye on you. It looks like I'll have to do this without your mother."

"If you say so."

"Lady Anthea! Sir Ash!" the Dark Fae king called.

Two knights approached the king, one of the knights being Lady Anthea. The other knight, with short brown hair and brown eyes, was dressed similarly, except the sword that he carried had leaves engraved on its hilt and tiny blue gemstones scattered across, and his wings, though similar to Lady Anthea's, were blue.

"Yes, your majesty?" Lady Anthea asked.

"I have to go and attend a court meeting, please keep an eye on Wisp."

"Of course, don't worry, your highness," both knights answered simultaneously as they left with the princess.

As soon as his daughter was out of sight, the Dark Fae king threw open the doors to the Northern Hall, a loud crash reverberated throughout the room.

Sparkling crystal chandeliers hung from the ceiling, giving off an ethereal glow. Banners in all colors and crests hung across the walls, representing the many courts in alliance with the Dark Fae Court. The shouts turned to hushed whispers as Oren stepped into the room in all his glory.

"What is going on? All you had to do was wait for a bit before I showed up, but you all decided to act like petulant children! Well? Is no one going to answer speak now?" Oren inquired.

"Greetings, your majesty," a calm voice echoed in the hall.

"Who said that?" Oren asked, looking around the room.

The calm voice came from the farthest end of the room, and the sea of allies parted so that Oren could get a better look at the individual speaking. She had light brown curly hair that barely touched her shoulders; her hazel-green eyes sparkled as if they were on fire. She wore a spring green dress decorated in white snowdrops, golden slippers on her feet, and hanging from her neck was a golden pendant, its shape forming a dragon.

"Greetings, my lady. You'll have to forgive me for the question, but who might you be?" Oren inquired.

"No need to worry, your majesty. This is my first time attending court. I'm Lady Aislyn, daughter of Dragon Lord Alaric and Queen Calista of the Shapeshifters. My father sends me on his behalf with a message for High Fae King Oren of the Dark Fae Court. He would like to join your alliance against the Light Fae and their allies due to a recent attack in his court."

"Welcome to your first meeting, Lady Aislyn. I don't mean to offend, but might I ask the reason your mother isn't attending?" asked Oren.

"I take no offense to this, your highness. My mother and father are no longer united. My mother has chosen the Light Fae's alliance and my father would like to join in your alliance's efforts to put a stop to them."

"Very well, Lady Aislyn, you and your father are more than welcome to attend court meetings whenever they may be called."

"I thank you, your majesty."

The Dark Fae king nodded, his gaze hardening as his eyes shifted toward the individuals in the room.

"Does anyone have a logical explanation as to why all of you were foolishly shouting like children?"

A moment of silence passed through the room filled with allies. No one dared to admit that they had been acting childishly.

"We have important matters to discuss. Next time, show some decorum and patience," the Dark Fae king said in response to the lack of response that he had received from his allies.

Nerida walked into the room as the little dragonflies on the wall danced in greeting. "Good morning, your majesty!" they chorused.

She placed a hand on Willow's forehead in a motherly fashion.

Willow's eyes flickered open, blinking blearily, unable to focus on the figure in front of her.

"Mom? Is that you?" Willow said longingly.

"No, sweetie. It's me, Nerida," the Dark Fae queen answered, her eyes filled with sadness for the young woman. Judging from the way she had called out for her mother, the Dark Fae queen could only assume that Willow hadn't seen her mother in quite some time.

Willow blinked furiously so that she could focus on the blurry figure in front of her.

"Nerida? My head hurts, and my mouth feels like sand from the desert. What happened?"

"The Light Fae attacked yesterday. More specifically, they tried to attack me and Oren. You saved me from getting attacked with powers no one knew you had. They seemed to have taken a toll on your body. There's also something else . . . " Nerida said, pausing in hesitation.

Willow felt nauseous and disoriented, but she was also curious as to why Nerida looked so hesitant.

"Oren wants you to attend a meeting with our allies because you were a witness when Heliodor attacked. He thinks that if you explain the attack, it would convince our allies that we aren't trying to cause trouble between realms."

Willow thought for a moment. It wasn't as though Oren had asked something particularly difficult of her. "That makes sense. When are you planning on calling everyone together for the meeting?"

"Well . . . it's today actually. I am most certain that all our allies have arrived for this meeting."

Willow's face went from thoughtful to shocked in a matter of seconds. "The meeting is today?"

"I told him it wasn't a good idea to do it so soon, but the sooner everyone knows about the threat, then the sooner we can do something about the Light Fae," Nerida offered.

"I need to get dressed first; I probably look terrible."

"You look fine, Willow, but if you want, there are spare clothes and shoes in the wardrobe. Just come outside in the hall when you're done changing. I will walk with you to the meeting."

As soon as Nerida stepped outside, Willow opened the dark-colored wardrobe and found herself face-to-face with dresses, tunics, and pants in all kinds of colors and designs. She pulled out a pale pink long-sleeved tunic with sleeves embroidered with silver leaves and a pair of gray pants. She shed her dusty rose sweater and black jeans and quickly pulled on the tunic and gray pants.

She grabbed a pair of tall black boots adorned with silver chains on the side and tugged them over her feet.

Satisfied, she grabbed a hairbrush from the nearby vanity and brushed through the tangled mess of her hair before tying it in to a ponytail with a black ribbon. Opening the door, she peered out into the hallway, "Nerida?"

"Wow! You look so pretty!"

Willow's cheeks heated up in embarrassment at Nerida's gushing. "Thank you."

"Let's go, or we'll really be late for the meeting."

They walked along the corridors, Nerida leading the way,

since Willow didn't know her way around the castle.

"Where is Oren holding the meeting?" Willow tried making small talk to quell her nerves.

"Usually, we hold it here in the castle, specifically in the Northern Hall."

"Will I have to say anything at this meeting?" Willow inquired.

"You don't have to tell them anything that you don't want to. The main purpose of the meeting is to discuss how the courts should prepare for a possible war. Some of our allies, they mean well, but not everyone is open and friendly. In any case, you're only attending because you were a witness to the attack that happened yesterday," explained Nerida.

They arrived at the double doors to the Northern Hall; loud shouts and yelling could be heard, mainly from Oren.

"It sounds lively in there," Willow said.

"I shouldn't be surprised. Lyndell can only do so much. Well, let's go inside."

Nerida and Willow threw open the double doors. All noise, even the whispers, stilled to a moment of eerie silence as the Dark Fae queen and her friend stepped through the doors to the awaiting audience of allies.

CHAPTER 3

"Who is that?" a questioning voice asked.

"Who invited a human to court?"

"That's not allowed!" another voice shouted in indignation.

"Silence!" a final voice thundered.

Once again, the sea of voices stilled to a hush, not a single soul uttering a word. No one wanted to incur the wrath of the Dark Fae king for fear of being thrown out, or worse, exiled from the alliance.

Oren took Willow's hand and helped her step up on the dais where he was standing.

"The first thing I would like to do is introduce a friend of mine. This is Willow Blackplum. She has saved my life and the life of my queen. Had she not done so, perhaps I would not be here today. She witnessed the attack that occurred yesterday involving the leader of the Light Fae, Heliodor."

"If Heliodor attacked, then how is it that you have no reported injuries, your majesty?" King Thistle asked. Thistle, the king of the Trolls, was the kind of person who didn't want to be in Oren's alliance, but at the insistence of his exuberant wife, Queen Nettle, he joined because she suggested it would be a way for Thistle to connect with the other courts in the realm and establish relationships.

His hair was bright orange, and it went down past his shoulders; his eyes were a muddy brown color. Hanging from around his neck was a silver medallion imprinted with a rock. He was dressed in dull gray robes that matched the tone of his home and of his skin. The Troll king wore no shoes, as individuals like him did not need them in the many caves and tunnel networks that made up his court. True to his namesake, he wore a bronze-colored crown in the shape of thistle flowers, each flower embedded with a malachite stone.

"Thistle! Have you no shame?" A figure who was dressed similarly to King Thistle, who Willow assumed was his wife, hissed at him to be silent. The only visual difference was that her crown had nettle leaves embedded with emeralds and her hair was a shock of white that stopped in a bob, while her eyes were an amber color.

"I am merely asking him. He expects us to believe that he was attacked in his own castle, and he brings in a human as a witness? Where is proof of that?" asked Thistle.

Lord Silverlight, the leader of the Unicorns, spoke out. "The individual that King Oren brought in is not a mere human. The magical energy coming from her is quite unique. That could possibly explain why no one was injured during the attack."

"Hah! If she's not a human, then why didn't King Oren say

anything about that when he introduced her?" questioned King Thistle.

"That is quite enough! I've tolerated you for the sake of your wife, King Thistle, but your behavior and attitude are unacceptable!" Oren bellowed. The shouting match between Oren and Thistle was starting to escalate far beyond what any of the other allies were expecting.

"Is anyone not the least bit concerned that the Dark Fae king has the audacity to say he was attacked and the only person to witness it is this mere human . . . creature . . . whatever she is? Not to mention the audacity of acting as if she's some hero? I'd be concerned if a random human was in this realm, seeing as how we ceased to communicate with their realm due to their own selfish desires," spat Thistle.

"What gives you the audacity as a ruler of a court to be disrespectful toward a guest? Much less act as if you are much better than the humans you say that you loathe!" demanded Oren.

It was clear to Willow that Oren would not tolerate Thistle's behavior in what was supposed to be a civilized meeting between the rulers of different courts.

"Oh, please, your majesty! Don't act as if you like humans any more than I do! We all know them to be selfish creatures!" Thistle retorted.

Willow would have kept silent and let King Thistle throw his little tantrum, but seeing the Troll king attack the Dark Fae king without a plausible cause stirred feelings of righteous fury.

Thus, the young woman spoke out against King Thistle's tirade.

"First and foremost, King Thistle," began Willow, "King Oren is not lying about being attacked. I was there when it happened. I don't think of myself as a hero, nor do I think myself stronger than anyone here. I saved the Dark Fae king because it was the right thing to do. Perhaps you should reflect on yourself instead of forming stereotypes about individuals you know nothing of. Instead of being relieved that he is alright and able to lead this meeting, you question his credibility? I didn't ask to come here; in fact, his majesty asked *me* to come here," Willow finished.

King Thistle scowled, his face twisting in anger. "Bah! Don't claim to be so innocent! If all this is true, why didn't the Dark Fae king mention that you have an air of magical energy about you? What does he stand to lose if he tells us about them?"

A voice interjected. "Would you not try to protect the people that you cared about? Have you ever thought that perhaps this would put Miss Blackplum in grave danger should anyone else discover her magical energy?"

Heads turned to see Prince Lyndell of the Moon Elf Court speak out. His raw-emerald-colored eyes stared back with equal intensity, daring anyone to disagree with him.

King Thistle scoffed. "What is the issue with telling us what creature of the realm she is? Is it some sort of secret? Perhaps it's one of the many secrets his majesty is keeping from us! The Dark Fae king is obviously hiding other things from us!" the Troll king shouted angrily.

"I've had just about enough of this nonsense! I didn't call this meeting so we could discuss miniscule matters. We have a more pressing matter at hand," Oren said, frustrated at the audacity

COURT OF THE DARK FAE

of King Thistle.

"Exactly! Stop asking King Oren such ridiculous questions and focus on the matters at hand!" Lyndell snapped.

"You're one to talk, Prince Lyndell. You are his oldest friend and therefore are most likely well informed of the situation," said King Thistle.

Ignoring the outburst of the Troll king, Oren pulled Nerida and Willow to the side.

Willow spoke out in a hushed tone to the two rulers.

"It seems as though King Thistle won't drop this issue unless he knows more about me."

The young woman's thoughts were running through her mind faster than she could register them. She'd been thrust into a world of magic and hadn't even known about her own powers until they had manifested during the attack that had happened the day before.

"This is ridiculous. It's obviously not an issue for him to be bringing it up now of all times. We have more pressing things to deal with," Nerida said, frustration washing over her already exhausted expression.

"He just wants the attention on something else rather than the issue at hand. How characteristically typical of him. That Troll would twist my words in a heartbeat just to prove that his idiotic assumption that I am hiding something is true," spat Oren.

The Dark Fae king seethed in anger, barely restraining his disdain over the Troll king.

"Then don't give him that opportunity. It doesn't matter if the court knows about my powers because that's not the real issue. It's only becoming an issue at King Thistle's insistence."

Past memories of her family yelling at her resurfaced. The pain from them was immeasurable and incomparable to the words that the Troll king spoke.

"Are you quite certain my dear? I don't want to put you in a difficult position," Oren asked with a soft expression.

"Don't worry about me. I can handle anything they decide to throw at me. He's the one putting you in a difficult position by ignoring everything else you have to say about attack carried out by the Light Fae," Willow replied.

"As you wish, my dear. I am less than thrilled to be telling him of all people, but his royal highness will only divide the alliance further with his big mouth."

"Maybe this time he'll stop talking or lose his voice from all of the screaming," muttered the Dark Fae queen.

Breaking up the conversation between the three of them, the Troll king interrupted.

"Are the three of you going to stand there and whisper your secret conversation amongst yourselves all day? Some of us have royal duties to attend to."

The Dark Fae king took a deep breath before addressing the group. "Yesterday, my queen and I were attacked by Heliodor. Had it not been for Miss Blackplum, perhaps Nerida would not be here. She manifested some sort of power when she saved us, leading to me to believe that she is not an ordinary individual."

"That is impossible! How can you suggest that someone like her can withstand the attack of a creature of this realm?"

demanded Thistle.

"That is none of your concern, King Thistle! How is it that you sit there and demand explanations, yet when presented with them, you continue to deny everything?"

"You haven't proven anything, your highness! All you've proven is that you are incapable of telling the truth!" Thistle replied.

"That is quite enough, Thistle. I don't think the high king has to prove anything, least of all to you. We have more pressing matters at hand, such as the possibility that the Light Fae are plotting a war," Queen Nettle said with a definitive tone. She motioned for her husband to sit down, not giving him a chance to further his attempts to undermine the high king and queen.

"I apologize on the behalf of my husband your majesties. He will not be coming here in the future. I will either come myself or send someone in my stead, as Lady Aislyn has done for her father."

"Your apology is appreciated, Queen Nettle. Now, as I have been saying since court started, we are in danger of being caught in a war with the Light Fae. I am certain Heliodor's attack on my castle is just the first of many. We need to be prepared for anything; do not trust anyone blindly," ordered Oren.

"Are you certain of this, high king?" This time, Queen Amaryllis, leader of the pixie folk, spoke out. She had long, flowing burgundy-colored hair. She wore a simple dress with no sleeves in a dark brown color, reminiscent of a tree trunk. Translucent wings imprinted with the designs of an unknown flower jutted out from her back. Green, leaf-like slippers that matched the tone of her skin completed her outfit. She wore no crown, for the pixie folk did not believe in such trinkets.

Her amethyst-colored eyes stared at the Fae king, issuing a silent challenge to his claims. "I'm quite certain. Heliodor would not have been so bold as to attack me in my own castle if they did not plan to go to war," Oren explained as calmly as he could, hoping that Queen Amaryllis wouldn't question him as much as King Thistle had.

Staring for a moment at the Dark Fae king, Queen Amaryllis nodded. "Very well. I shall take your word for it, high king."

Oren scanned the room briefly. "Court is adjourned for today. I strongly advise everyone present to remain on guard," he declared.

As soon as the high king finished speaking and the members of the alliance left, King Thistle stood up abruptly despite his wife's protests.

"Thistle! You've embarrassed our court quite enough, have you no shame? We should be leaving like everyone else!" his wife yelled as he began to walk away from her.

"I am allowed to speak my mind, am I not? This was a highly irregular meeting and a complete waste of time! How can you stand there as the high king and spout such ridiculous conspiracies of war? Where is your proof? One attack and apparently they're plotting war!" bellowed Thistle.

Willow interjected, having heard enough of King Thistle's outrageous outbursts. "He tried to murder the high king and queen. What kind of proof are you looking for? A dead body?"

"You're one to talk. You think you can come here and win King

Oren's favor by saving his life and the life of Queen Nerida? By acting as if you are something other than a human?" Thistle spat.

The Dark Fae king responded before Willow could continue, he hadn't meant to drag her into the petty rivalry that King Thistle seemed to have with him. "There you go again, bringing up something that had nothing to do with the purpose of this meeting. I honestly cannot fathom why you think whether Willow is an actual Faeling or just a human is the main issue here. Or why you seem to think that I am giving her some sort of special treatment. Clearly, you have such grand delusions that are preventing you from thinking straight. The main issue, King Thistle, if you bothered to listen, is that our alliance could be at risk. Now, if you'll excuse me, I have more important matters to attend to." His last point had been made. It was clear to Willow that Oren was done playing the stupid mind games that the Troll king wanted to play.

"I'm not through with you, high king! I want to know exactly what you're hiding from me and from the rest of the alliance," bellowed Thistle.

"You better not talk to him that way!" Lyndell was furious with the way the Troll king was speaking to his friend. "King Oren doesn't have to explain personal matters to you!"

"Calm yourself, Prince Lyndell," interjected Oren. "King Thistle, I would watch the tone with which you are speaking to me. I don't have to explain personal matters to you, as Prince Lyndell has pointed out. Now tell me this, what's to stop me from barring you from the alliance, hmm?"

"You think you're so clever just because you're the high king, don't you your highness?" the Troll king spat bitterly.

"Thistle! That's enough out of your mouth! I will not tolerate this kind of behavior from you, how could you disrespect the high king like that in front of me? You are lucky that no one from the alliance is here right now! I deeply apologize for everything, King Oren; his behavior is quite unacceptable, and I will do everything in my power to make sure he does not attend any meetings in the future," Queen Nettle shared.

"You shouldn't have to apologize for his incompetence. But, nevertheless, I appreciate the apology. Excuse me," Oren said as he made his way toward the door.

Lyndell, Nerida, and Willow bid the Troll queen farewell and followed Oren out of the hall.

"That was a nightmare!" Lyndell said in the hallway.

"Thank you, Lyndell, for stating the obvious fact," Nerida said as she shook her head in obvious annoyance.

"King Thistle can be a very dangerous individual. The way he proceeded to undermine my attempts to warn our allies of an impending war speaks volumes. I don't know why I tolerated that fool for so long!" The Dark Fae king's inner frustrations were beginning to show. He had dealt with the Troll king for as long as he had formed the alliance. Each time, instead of being an ally, the Troll king had become an instigator with his ceaseless questions to find out the supposed truth that was being hidden from him.

"We all know his wife is the one who's really in charge of the court. Otherwise, his lovely little court would be in ruins with the way he speaks and belittles others," Nerida shared. She was beyond agitated, and that was quite rare for the usually cheerful Dark Fae queen.

"On the bright side, at least he won't be coming to any future meetings between the courts. Queen Nettle said she'd send someone else in her place if she couldn't come," chimed Lyndell, attempting to boost the mood.

"Let's hope that she sends someone who is capable and not so argumentative," said Willow, attempting to infuse positivity into the situation to buoy her newfound friends' outlook.

The conversation was interrupted by the arrival of a guard who came rushing in at the same time as Sir Ash and Lady Anthea with Princess Wisp in tow.

"Your majesties! Something has happened in the dungeons! Heliodor has escaped!" shouted a guard with silver-colored hair.

"It's true, your majesty! Sir Ash and I were looking after the princess when the news broke. We rushed over as soon as we could," Lady Anthea said in a rushed tone.

"We were caught unaware your majesty. He escaped. I gave strict orders to the rotation of guards to make sure that he was very securely guarded. I don't know how this happened," Adair said, scrambling for a way to placate the oncoming onslaught of Oren's anger.

"Lady Anthea, Sir Ash, take my daughter to her room," ordered Oren.

"Yes, your highness," they both answered simultaneously, taking the princess off in the other direction.

As soon as they were out of sight, the Dark Fae king turned all of his fury on the guard who had alerted him about Heliodor's escape, albeit a little too late.

"Tell me something, Adair. You are the captain of the guard, are you not? A supposedly capable individual, chosen for his skills and abilities? How is it that you let someone of lesser power escape? All you had to do was keep watch over the dungeons until the meeting concluded! Did it not occur to you that perhaps this was an emergency for which you could interrupt the meeting? Of all the other times that you have interrupted me, you thought it was prudent to stay silent now? Get out of my sight and do not come back here! If I find out you are solely responsible for Heliodor's escape, you'll find yourself as a permanent guest in my dungeons!" With much irritation, the Dark Fae king turned on his heel and walked away, the threat hanging in the air and the tension quite palpable. This gave way for the Dark Fae queen to rip into the captain of the guard.

"Heliodor got away and no one thought to alert us? What kind of ridiculous act are you running, Adair? Do you have an inkling of common sense, or have you lost it all? What if he comes after Wisp or Willow? Are you not second in power to Oren when it comes to guarding this castle and its inhabitants? How can you stand there and make excuses?" The Dark Fae queen was beyond livid. Someone who had tried to kill both her and the Fae king was now running lose once more, free to plot against the Dark Fae Court again. Adair, already humiliated by the Dark Fae king, decided that it was the best time to continue making excuses.

"I made a mistake, your highness. I don't understand why you are accusing me of being reckless," he argued.

Lyndell spoke out, he was getting tired of the Fae's excuses and disrespect toward the Fae rulers. "Surely you jest! If I were you, Adair, I would seriously reconsider my tone, because if Oren doesn't find cause to throw you in the dungeons, then I most certainly will. You should leave, *now*."

Adair turned on his heel and quickly walked away, both threats from both rulers ringing clearly in his mind.

"Sorry you had to see that, Willow. Adair's behavior right now was quite erratic, he's never failed to perform his duties properly," shared the queen.

"It's alright, Nerida. I don't blame you, especially after having to deal with the Troll king."

"Don't remind me," interrupted the Moon Elf prince. "He's so annoying! We should find Oren; he might break something if he hasn't already."

Willow stifled a laugh at Lyndell's statement. "Break something? You say that like it's a common occurrence."

His sheepish smile was all she needed to see to confirm that this was indeed a common occurrence with the Fae king. The trio all left to find the disgruntled Dark Fae king, unaware that the traitor in their midst was plotting his revenge.

Later on, in the comfort of her room, Willow was left with the cacophony of thoughts that threatened to consume her mind. She hadn't even the chance to breathe before being whisked away by Nerida to a meeting between alliances.

For most of her life, she had thought of herself as no one special, going about her days just as anyone else would. She lived her life in a normal way, going to school and work, coming back home to an empty apartment. Every day was a mundane occurrence, but within the span of a few hours after meeting the Dark Fae king, everything had changed.

The young woman, having just met Nerida, was willing to sacrifice her own life and in turn discovered that she had powers. She could no longer consider herself to be normal, let alone a human. What human had magical powers to begin with?

Then there was something that had been sitting in the back of her mind, an idea that was trying to fight its way to the surface. If she had powers, what was the reasoning her parents might've used in keeping that a secret from her? Of course, their relationship started to deteriorate after a certain point in their lives, yet they had some time to let her know about something of this magnitude.

All her life, she had been thought of as weird and unusual. No matter where she went, or who she thought she had become friends with, everyone was the same. If they needed something, they would talk to her and act like the best of friends. If they no longer needed her, it was back to talking about her behind her back. When she was still with her family, she felt that they didn't take an interest in her hobbies or support her dreams.

But here, especially in Oren's court, he had seemingly welcomed her, treated her with courtesy and respect. He made her feel like she belonged somewhere, even if she was a human. If even for a moment these feelings were fleeting, she would still cherish them forever.

CHAPTER 4

Gray, dreary, and dimly lit halls. The only glow came from a black crystal chandelier, orange flames flickering from each of the candles in each holder. An individual sat poised on her throne like a statue; her cold, crimson and gold eyes staring down at the figure bowing in front of her. Her onyx hair fell down like a curtain behind her, a crown of black thorns encircled her head, amber stones nestled in random spots. Many silver rings with the same stone littered her fingers. Dressed in an olive-colored dress with black-heeled shoes, she made for an intimidating figure. The dimly lit room did not conceal her displeasure toward the person on the ground in front of her.

"Why are you here, Heliodor? In case it wasn't obvious, I am quite displeased with you. You've failed twice thus far to kill the Fae king, and you managed to get captured this time. Tell me, why should I hide you here, in the Dwarf court?" the woman spat toward the floor.

"Queen Nessa, while I have failed to kill Oren, I've uncovered a few secrets. I have a spy on the inside, of which the Dark Fae king is unaware. He will give *you* intelligence when I am unable to collect it from him," Heliodor shared.

"Oh? And what new information do you have pertaining to the Dark Fae king that I don't already have?" she inquired. Nessa wasn't a patient individual, and Heliodor's failures only served to worsen her mood.

"Oren has let a Faeling stay in his court. At least, I believe she may be one. She saved not only his life, but that of his wretched queen as well." Heliodor's tone crept toward pleading, as if he knew his fate was hanging on the queen finding his information valuable.

"Interesting, I was sure that the last of the Faelings had gone and died out. This supposed Faeling, did you manage to get her name? Where did she come from?" she asked.

"She goes by the name Willow. Before meeting the Fae king, I believe she resided somewhere in the human realm. As for where, I have yet to discover that. Her magical abilities are far from that of a normal Faeling, she was able to wrap me in ropes made from pure magic!"

"I want you to get more information about this Faeling, Heliodor. She may prove to be a useful tool in the destruction of the Dark Fae Court and the downfall of King Oren. If she was powerful enough to stop you, then she may be powerful enough to stop Oren as well." Nessa paused, looking at Heliodor thoughtfully. "And what of the Dark Fae king's alliance?" The gears were turning in the Dwarf queen's head, plotting with the information she had just received.

"The Dragon lord has decided to ally himself with them and

sent his daughter to confirm the alliance. Because his former wife, Queen Calista, seeks to ally herself with us. Lord Alaric has deemed that unacceptable in his eyes and instead of remaining neutral, has decided to pledge his support to the Dark Fae Court," Heliodor said at a rapid pace, attempting to win more of Nessa's favor.

"Such a pity. They could have been our most useful allies. Nevertheless, I have no doubt that the Shapeshifter queen will be attending the meeting today. She may be difficult to convince given that her husband and daughter have both joined Oren's alliance. But even so, the sharpest of weapons can be dulled," she continued.

"What then, my queen? What will we do after we convince Queen Calista to join us?" he asked. Queen Nessa smirked; this was why she was in charge of this whole plot. Bumbling fools like Heliodor couldn't possibly fathom the extent her influence reached.

"That, my dear Light Fae, is quite obvious. We, rather *you*, are going to convince Oren's little friend to betray him and join our cause. Once we deal him that blow, he'll be too busy wallowing in self-pity to pay any attention to the chaos around him. That's when we shall strike and rid the realm of him—permanently!"

They both chuckled darkly, because to them, the Dark Fae king's days were numbered. Even more so if they managed to convince the Faeling to join them.

"Well, don't just stand here and laugh, go and call our meeting!" Nessa said, interrupting Heliodor.

"Right away, my queen," he said just before scurrying off.

Not more than a moment had passed after Heliodor sent the call out for a meeting that the prince of the Sun Elves arrived. Prince Sol, whose beauty shined just as the sun did, had waist-length hair the color of clouds on a sunny day and eyes a bright, sky-blue color. He was dressed in a golden tunic with dark blue pants and matching shoes, on the top of his head rested a golden crown emblazoned with suns decorated with an emerald jewel embedded in the center. He sneered at the dark, dimly lit halls of Nessa's castle.

"I see the halls haven't changed a bit," he remarked. "One would think that Queen Nessa would have had the sense to add some light in this dreary place."

"I see you're still as uptight as ever, Prince Sol. Perhaps you should loosen up, we are plotting to go to war with your cousins after all," smarted Heliodor.

"Ah, Heliodor. So, you're still running around as Queen Nessa's errand boy. And you still haven't managed to kill the Dark Fae king. Such a pity, and here I thought you were an accomplished individual," he said.

"You call yourself the leader of the Sun Elves, yet you're still a prince, Sol. So really, who's the failure here?" retorted Heliodor.

"I didn't overthrow the leader of my people unlike you, Heliodor! They can't even call you their king because you failed to follow the proper protocols."

A shower of glitter and lights appeared, blinding the Sun Elf prince and Light Fae.

With a flourish, an individual stepped into view. He had sun-kissed skin, long blond locks framed his face and reached down to his waist; highlights of silver and red could be plainly seen on various parts of his hair, his eyes were a blood-red color. He wore a glittery, crimson-colored tailcoat over a gray-colored poet's shirt with black pants. Tall, heeled, dark gray boots with black chains hanging from the sides completed his outfit. He wore a singular silver pendant around his neck in the shape of a silver lily.

By his side was someone with waist-length, dark brown hair that fell down her back in a braid, a wreath of white lilies sat on her head as a sort of crown. She wore a lilac-colored gown that flared out with many layers, the embroidery designed to look like lilies, completed with silver slippers. Silver earrings dangled from her ears, their shape forming a solid circle with an amethyst in the middle. Much like the individual next to her, she wore a matching silver lily pendant.

"I see you idiots are still at each other's throats," the Goblin king remarked smoothly.

"Ah, King Nash. How are your Goblins doing? Are they perhaps still playing house in your little fortress?" jeered the Sun Elf prince.

"Living in a fortress doesn't mean that we are unaware of events that transpire on the outside, Prince Sol. You would do well to remember that," said Nash.

"Your threats are just as pathetic as your subjects if not more. Don't think you can threaten me, Goblin king!"

"Watch your tone, elf. Need I remind you that between both of our courts, mine know how to fight better than yours." The stare that the Goblin king sent Prince Sol's way sent shivers down the prince's spine, though he would never admit to such a thing;

his kind were very prideful, after all.

King Nash was the leader of the Goblins, and although his appearance stated otherwise, he was still an intimidating figure, standing at least a few feet taller than the Sun Elf prince. The most unique thing about his appearance was that whilst most Goblins had skin in different shades of green, their king and his queen were the exceptions to that rule.

"I heard you couldn't even get rid of the Dark Fae king, Heliodor. I'd save the childish arguments for when you're actually successful," scoffed the woman next to the Goblin king.

This woman was King Nash's wife, Queen Hellia. She was a human, although her true identity was a secret to all who knew them. Hellia had had been abandoned by her family as a young child. She was found and raised by the Goblins in his court. When he met her by chance, he'd fallen head over heels for her and after courting her, they wed.

"What would you know about the difficulties of killing the Dark Fae king, hmm? It's not as easy to kill Oren as you think it is, Queen Hellia. If he hadn't been found by that girl, I would have finished him and perhaps even his entire family!"

Queen Nessa walked out of her throne room before anyone else could respond, her intense gaze landing on every individual present in the halls.

"The Gnomes will not be joining us because they're dealing with personal issues. Let's convene in Malachite Hall today."

The entire alliance followed Nessa to Malachite Hall. It was just as dimly lit as the rest of Nessa's castle. A black-jeweled chandelier hung from the ceiling; the walls were lined with plain gray tapestries decorated with silhouettes of silver leaves. A high dais was positioned in the center of the room, a singular throne resting on top. As Queen Nessa stood up on the dais, the room turned deadly silent, so much so that you could hear a feather drop.

"Now that I have your attention, let's attend to business. The first thing I'd like to address is Heliodor's failure in eliminating the Dark Fae king. He was given many opportunities to do so, including a few days ago when the Dark Fae king was in the human realm. Oren is also housing a Faeling in his court. You must be thinking that it's impossible for such an individual to exist, but she is the reason that Heliodor failed in his pitiful attempt to kill the Dark Fae king."

The Goblin king snickered at this and promptly interrupted the Dwarf queen. "If I may interject, Queen Nessa, why is Heliodor being put in charge of eliminating Oren? He's clearly not cut out for the job."

"Shut your mouth, Nash! I would have been able to kill him if he hadn't been saved by that Faeling. They aren't even supposed to exist; the last one died out long ago! Her magic is nothing like a normal Fae's," Heliodor defended.

"Having a little meltdown are we, Heliodor? I wouldn't make excuses to justify my failure. If the Faeling exists as you say, then where is she, hmm? Your excuses would be valid if you actually had proof to back your claims." The Goblin king knew very well that Heliodor could not control his anger, and he was hoping to agitate a response out of him. For far too long, Queen Nessa treated Heliodor as if he were a hero after getting rid of King Faven. The many dark tasks that the Dwarf queen had entrusted

Heliodor with could have easily been done by Nash with speed and precision.

That was his reasoning for baiting the Light Fae after all. What better way to show how awful Heliodor was than to make him look unintelligent in front of the Dwarf queen?

Heliodor knew that Nash was being purposefully impudent, yet his ego and desire to gain some sort of approval from Nessa outweighed any inkling of sense that he might possess. After all, he was the one that managed to gain a spy in Oren's castle.

"You are a complete idiot, Nash," retorted Heliodor. "Why should I have to prove to you that she exists? You're not the one who ended up in Oren's dungeon, nor were you defeated by a Faeling!"

Prince Sol interrupted their little quarrel. It was only amusing until it became irritating. "I fail to see how that is of any importance. Why not deal a deeper blow to Oren? We should turn the Faeling over to our side. She's apparently powerful enough to subdue Heliodor, and she may be a valuable asset to our alliance in the future."

Nessa decided to intervene in the discussions, lest the members of the alliance start to take credit for her devious plans. She was the one in charge.

"If she is indeed a Faeling, then perhaps she may be the key to the destruction of Oren and his court," said Nessa. "We may not need to kill him after all. A blow from a trusted friend or ally is much more severe versus a blow from a complete enemy. With an astounding stroke of luck, Heliodor was able to plant a spy within the castle and retrieve the information pertaining to the

Faeling. The Faeling is indeed very powerful; her magic runs far stronger than any Faeling that anyone has ever seen in a lifetime."

"Why do we need to destroy the Dark Fae king and take his court? Are all of you not satisfied with the positions of power you're already in? Of course, I don't really care what you simpletons do. I'm only here for my own amusement," a stoic yet amused voice called out.

Heads turned to see that the statement had come from someone who looked like they did not want to be here yet decided to come for amusement's sake.

Lord Obsidian, the lord of the Gnomes, was the one who had spoken this bold statement to the Dwarf queen. Tossing his forest-colored hair out of his face, his ink-black eyes stared at everyone inside the hall. Wearing a simple green tunic and pants with black riding boots and a silver sword on his hip, he painted the very picture of intimidation.

"Ah, Lord Obsidian. I see that you've finally decided to show your face despite the personal issue you had to take care of. And in your most plain clothes as well. How charming," broke in Nessa. "As for your statement, for far too long, the Dark Fae king has been the high king of this entire realm. Have any of you fools bothered to look at his title? He is literally in charge of all the courts! How is that fair to any of us?"

Nessa's answer did not satisfy the Gnome lord in the slightest, although he was supposedly a neutral figure, having never associated with any particular side of the realm. Ignoring the jab at his appearance, he decided to answer.

"Has he ever done anything to make the rest of you seem

small and insignificant?" questioned Obsidian. "Most of the time, he is in his own court, taking care of matters related to that. And not only that, but he does pay attention to certain situations in each court, much more than any of you who call yourselves rulers do." Obsidian paused, looking at each of them to see if they had a response. "If I may be bolder than I already am, he's much more of a leader than any of you sitting here are. He not only takes care of matters in secret for you all, but he does not boast about it, nor does he hold it over you. You want to go to war and kill the one individual in the realm that is actually helping you." He paused again; still, there were no rebuttals. "I may be neutral, but even I'm not so foolish as to believe one side of a story over the other. You have not provided a single soul in this room reasonable proof or solid arguments for why you want to kill the Dark Fae king, myself included."

Nessa did not want to deal with the Gnome lord. If he started making the members of the Light Alliance question her, then she would lose support, and in turn lose the chance to be the high queen of the realm. Turning her head toward the rest of the members in the meeting, Nessa chose to ignore him in favor of other things.

"Today we have a special guest joining us, Queen Callista of the Shapeshifters." Queen Nessa gestured to a figure hidden in the shadows who came forward. Long, dark, crimson-colored hair fell past the figure's shoulders, spilling down in waves, eyes sparkling in an intense olive color.

The figure wore a sparkling gold dress with matching heels; gold chandelier earrings dangled from her ears and many golden bracelets adorned her wrists. A golden crown with geometric designs sat on her head, embedded with topaz gems.

She spoke in voice that dripped like honey, though perhaps a bit too sweet, like she was hiding something. "It's quite a pleasure to be here today." The words slid out of her mouth slowly and seductively. "It is with regret that I am without my husband or my daughter, as they have decided to join that wretched Dark Fae king's alliance. However, myself and my subjects are at your disposal, Queen Nessa." Queen Callista, after her introduction and declaration of loyalty, sat down while Queen Nessa spoke again.

"Thank you, Queen Callista. Your pledge of loyalty is greatly appreciated. It is unfortunate that your husband and daughter are not here with you. I am however pleased that you came to your senses regarding Oren. Our meeting is adjourned for today. I will send a message for the next meeting. Until then, I will work on getting the Faeling over to our side. We will go from there and coordinate a plan to destroy the Dark Fae Court and their allies."

Cheers erupted as Nessa stepped down from the dais and left the room, all of her allies following suit.

It was indeed a dark day; one could only hope that things wouldn't get worse.

CHAPTER 5

It has always been a dangerous sentiment to keep your enemies close to you. After all, they are the ones who want to cause your downfall. Fortunately, the one echoing this statement was none other than the Dark Fae king.

By demoting his captain of the guard to a lower rank, not only was King Oren keeping a known spy close, but he was able to throw Adair off guard, so to speak.

For now, Adair was content that he was still allowed in the castle and therefore could still be a spy for Heliodor. Adair was known to be a very prideful and arrogant Dark Fae, perhaps even more so than the Fae king himself. He had silver-colored hair that fell down to his shoulders and heterochromatic eyes in the colors of silver and violet.

His face held a cruel, calculated, and cold gaze. His silver armor was decorated with crab blossoms embedded with pink-and-white gemstones, a silver sword hanging from a scabbard on his hip. Much like the rest of the Dark Fae in the court, he had butterfly-like wings, violet in color with black-and-white dots scattered across.

While Adair was perhaps celebrating the fact that he had not been thrown out of the castle and could potentially still spy for Heliodor, the Dark Fae king was seething silently at Heliodor's escape. Willow and Lyndell were silently sitting with the Dark Fae king, both unsure of what to say, while Nerida had gone off with Wisp to see if they could perhaps make something for the evening meal, that is, if Oren still had an appetite after dealing with Adair.

The room they were in held tones of blue and gray, the seats and cushions matching the color scheme of the room, save for the purple dragonflies and butterflies that were embroidered on each cushion. In the far corner of the room, a fireplace gave off a warm glow, though that did nothing to ease the stress and tension in the room.

"I'd like to know why you're demoting Adair and not actually getting rid of him. Do you have any idea how dangerous of a person he really is? He just let Heliodor escape! Doesn't that make you the least bit concerned? You do realize that he can make shadow keys, right?" Lyndell said, finally breaking the silence. His concern for his friend outweighed any fear he had of being caught in the Dark Fae king's wrath.

"You really have a way with words, don't you? Do you honestly think that I am stupid enough that I don't know anything about Adair? I know he's a spy for the other alliance; after all, he is powerful enough to subdue Heliodor. And outing him now would only serve to further complicate the matter. Why in the realm do you think I chose Adair to be captain of the guard? It certainly wasn't just for show."

Prince Lyndell rubbed the back of his head, embarrassed for having told off his friend when he was more than aware of the situation. Willow decided to interrupt. She didn't want the Dark Fae king to lose his temper over a trivial explanation of why he'd decided to keep a spy in his employ.

"What exactly is a shadow key?"

"A shadow key can open any lock or door in this realm. Only a few Fae, such as myself, are able to make them for the ability is quite rare," explained Oren.

Willow thought for a moment before speaking; that kind of key sounded familiar to her. "It sounds similar to a skeleton key. Although a skeleton key can only open one type of lock as opposed to shadow keys."

Lyndell, interrupted his friend before he could respond, "I know you're aware of the situation, Oren, but don't you think it's dangerous to continue to let Adair stay in the castle?"

Oren scoffed. "If you must know, Lyndell, by keeping Adair in the castle, I am able to closely monitor his movements. Make no mistake, he will suffer the consequences of his actions, and I will do whatever it takes to make sure that Nessa meets her untimely demise."

Lyndell sighed, perhaps he shouldn't have been so outspoken or harsh with his friend. "I suppose I should have known that you have your reasons for doing things."

Oren rolled his eyes at his idiotic friend. "That is the worst apology you can give me for your unimpressive outburst,

Lyndell. However, I guess I'll take what I can get."

Willow playfully rolled her eyes at the two rulers and their antics. But one thing was still bothering her: If Adair was still in the castle, what were the chances that he wasn't listening to any and all conversations that occurred? "You don't think Adair's listening in on our conversation, do you?"

Oren chuckled at Willow's question, after all, he didn't do things without reason. "Actually, Willow, this is one of those rooms that Adair isn't able to find. I imbued a powerful spell that only allows individuals whom I trust to find this room."

Nerida and Wisp walked into the room before Willow or Lyndell could respond to the Fae king.

"Dinner is ready. The royal chef and I made all your favorites, Oren," the Dark Fae queen proclaimed.

But, before the Dark Fae queen could say anything else, Oren walked out of the room.

"I guess Dad was hungry," Wisp chirped. Lyndell, Willow, and Nerida collectively laughed at Wisp's statement and left the room to join the Fae king. The four of them arrived in the dining room to find an impatient, irritated, and probably very hungry Dark Fae king sitting in his usual seat.

"You look hungry, Oren," Lyndell said. If looks could instantly kill, the Moon Elf prince would've been dead, especially with the way the Dark Fae king glared at him.

"How could you tell, Red?" The ever-sarcastic Dark Fae king was getting irritated with his friend.

The spread in front of them looked incredible, from the strange blue soup to the salad that had a rainbow of vegetables, to the many sandwiches piled high on large plates. Desserts ranging from a strawberry cheesecake to cookies to strawberry pudding were laid out on the large table. Nerida, Oren, Lyndell, Willow, and Wisp all sat down around the table and ate the delicious meal.

Lyndell bit into his sandwich, albeit a little too hard as the contents splattered all over Oren's face. The color drained from the Moon Elf prince's face.

"Oh dear . . . I'm sorry, Oren!" he cried.

The Dark Fae king wiped his face before he stood up and grabbed a bowl of strawberry pudding. Walking calmly over to Prince Lyndell, he smashed his face into the pudding.

"I said I was sorry!" whined the prince.

"Next time, eat your food away from my face, you menace," Oren said simply as he went back to drinking his soup.

The Moon Elf prince huffed as he wiped the sticky mess from his face.

"Oren, stop setting a bad example for Wisp and apologize to Lyndell at once," Nerida said in a stern tone, leaving no room for argument.

Sighing in exasperation, he turned to his friend.

"I'm sorry, Red."

After that little exchange, they finished eating their meal. Lyndell stood up and with a dramatic flourish, bid everyone a good night, and left for his own court.

"Goodbye, everyone! See you tomorrow, Oren!" he shouted over his shoulder as he walked out. It was obvious the Dark Fae king hoped Lyndell wouldn't show up in the morning—that would mean more noise, more broken vases, and less sleep.

"I'll go and make some tea." The Dark Fae queen got up from the table and headed toward the kitchen with Wisp trailing after her. It was then that Oren decided to bring up something that had been eating away at his thoughts.

"If I may ask you something, Willow, why is it that your parents believed the words of someone who had no proof over your own? Of course, if you are not comfortable with answering such a question, then I have no qualms."

Willow, taken aback at the question, softly sighed. Her sister wasn't someone she liked to talk about, but she also knew that Oren didn't mean any harm in asking.

"My sister, Aerina, has always been the golden child for as long as I can remember. She can say and do anything, and my parents will still adore her. But the main reason my parents never listened to me whenever I had a complaint about her is because she made them see me as a disrespectful and dishonest person. She told them about my friends, and of course my parents didn't want to listen to anything I had to say afterwards."

"I'm sorry you had to go through that, my dear. Forgive me for saying so, but your sister sounds awful," Oren said.

Willow shrugged her shoulders; she didn't make her sister the way she was, and there was obviously no way she would change either. "It's alright, Oren. I can't change what's happened to me in the past. I can only focus on what will happen in the future."

Before the Dark Fae king could respond, Nerida and Wisp came back with tea, and much to the delight of the Dark Fae king and Willow, they also had a tray of strawberry cookies.

"I brought the cookies for you, Dad. I know how much you like to eat them when Mom isn't in the kitchen," Wisp said with a sneaky smile.

Nerida and Willow burst out in laughter as the Dark Fae king's expression showed that he was utterly flabbergasted and defeated by his little daughter. "I don't eat them all the time, Wisp."

He had to think of something before he got into trouble with Nerida; she'd never let him hear the end of it.

"You know, Nerida, all you have to do is replace the cookies with vegetables, then he won't be eating so many," Willow said laughing.

The Dark Fae queen chuckled. "I think that's a wonderful idea, sweetie."

The Fae king gave the both of them an unamused stare as he sipped his tea. "You two must believe that you're an absolute dream team," he quipped.

"Maybe Nerida and I should dethrone you then." Willow tried and failed to smother a laugh at the face Oren was making.

"I will get you back for that Miss Blackplum. For now, I'll let your teasing slide."

A yawn from Wisp distracted the Dark Fae queen and Willow from responding; after all it had been a taxing day for everyone. "Come on, Wisp, let's get you to bed, sweetie. You can talk with Willow in the morning." The Dark Fae queen knew that Wisp wanted to stay up so she could talk to Willow, but it was getting quite late, and the little Dark Fae princess needed to get some sleep.

The Dark Fae princess walked up to her father and gave him a hug, then she turned to Willow and did the same thing.

"Goodnight, Dad and Willow. See you tomorrow!"

"Goodnight my little flower petal, sweet dreams."

"Goodnight, Wisp. I can't wait to spend some time with you tomorrow!" exclaimed Willow.

As soon as Nerida left with Wisp, Oren stood up and offered his arm to Willow, and together they walked out on to a nearby balcony.

The stars glistened in the dark night sky like thousands of tiny diamonds, and some of the stars formed constellations that danced around the sky, even more so when they saw the Dark Fae king.

"The night sky here is so beautiful. I didn't think the constellations would actually move," Willow reflected.

"Yes, they do that every single night . . . when it's clear, of course. I take it that doesn't happen in the human realm?" he asked.

"Not really, I mean, the stars do make constellations, but they certainly don't dance around like this."

Nerida joined them a few moments later, having put Wisp to bed. The three of them stood content on the balcony, watching the beautiful stars and constellations, and enjoying a peaceful moment. But Willow wondered how long moments like these would last? With the potential threats of war and spies looming over them, moments such as these would become scarce.

CHAPTER 6

As everyone in the castle slumbered, a golden mist passed through the doors. The sickly sweet scent of nightshade filled the air, rendering the guards unconscious. The mist floated toward Willow's room, dissipating to reveal the same curtain of golden hair and fiery orange eyes. Dressed in golden armor decorated with the same sun pattern on his sword, there stood Heliodor in all his despicable glory. He'd just cast a spell that would leave the guards unconscious long enough for him to capture the young woman inside the room.

Heliodor turned the handle on the door, but much to his chagrin, the door creaked. Willow stirred from the noise, awakening from her deep sleep. She turned her head toward the door, then got up out of bed slowly. She grabbed a small dagger from underneath her pillow; something Oren had given her before they parted ways to sleep.

"I suppose you think you're so clever, Faeling. Hiding a weapon that you cannot even use and trying to wield it against me." Heliodor thought that scathing remark would perhaps ignite an indignation within Willow and cause her to attack him blindly. Unfortunately for him, Willow wasn't one for falling victim to his ridiculous insults.

"You might be able to trick others with that ridiculous statement, but you are sadly mistaken if you think that tactic will work on me," responded Willow. She readied the dagger in her hands; she couldn't attack Heliodor with such a small weapon, but she could definitely defend herself.

"I hope you don't think your precious Dark Fae king will come to your rescue should you manage to succeed in defending yourself against me. The moment I stepped into this room, all sounds ceased to be heard from anyone on the outside."

Unbeknownst to Heliodor, the black, silhouetted dragonflies on the wall heard his every word and rushed off to find Oren. Heliodor smirked at Willow and charged at her with a silver scimitar.

The clashing sound of the scimitar hitting the walls and the furniture cut through the air as Willow clumsily dodged each attack coming from Heliodor. Unfortunately, she wasn't well versed in combat, thus her constant dodging was making her tired.

In a moment of brief intermission, she tried to focus, hoping that her powers would somehow manifest the same way they did when she defended Nerida. A few silver sparks left her fingertips, but unlike the first time where her powers had left Heliodor immobile, this spark of power wasn't enough to do any harm to him. Noticing her plight, Heliodor laughed darkly and tried to attack her with much more force than before. Willow, barely dodging his attack, breathed heavily, her expression turning fearful as she realized the Light Fae would best her in battle after all.

"I expected more of a fight from you! Were you not the one who had me bound in your own magic? Did you expect to best me in a fight? How pathetic!" Heliodor screamed.

Whilst the battle was going on in Willow's room, the dragonflies finally made it to Oren's quarters, their buzzing voices waking him up.

"What in the realm is going on? Stop chattering all at once and speak one at a time!" Oren demanded. Oren was half asleep and fully irritated.

"Willow is in danger! Heliodor is back and he's attacking her!" one of the dragonflies shared quickly. Oren threw his covers back and ran to the door a moment later; he hoped to make it to Willow's room before Heliodor was able to do serious harm.

Heliodor elbowed Willow in the stomach, his eyes holding an evil glint as he watched her fail to block his blow, the dagger finally falling out of her hands and clattering to the floor.

While pointing his scimitar to Willow's throat, he wished he could take revenge on her for his humiliation the day before. It was a pity that the Dwarf queen ordered him to bring her back unharmed.

Instead, he used his magic to create the same golden, sickly sweet, nightshade-scented mist into her face that had rendered the guards unconscious. Willow covered her face and nose in an attempt to not inhale the mist, but her efforts were in vain as she fell unconscious, her body hitting the floor. Satisfied with his work, the Light Fae slung her unconscious body over his shoulder and walked over to the window.

With a tap of his finger, the glass cracked and turned to dust before hitting the ground.

He flew out the paneless window and headed in the direction of Nessa's castle, Willow still hanging limp over his shoulder.

A moment later, Oren burst into the room. He looked around. Furniture was toppled and wall decorations were broken and laying on the floor—it was clear a struggle had just occurred. He noticed the dust around the window, a slight breeze was wafting in, highlighting Heliodor's escape route. The Dark Fae king stepped out into the hallway; a handful of his men were laying lifeless on the castle floor. He smelled the nightshade lingering in the air. Using his magic, a sapphire mist left his hands, and the pleasant scent of rhododendrons replaced the unpleasant scent of nightshade, rousing his guards from their slumber.

"What in the realm happened? Who let Heliodor back into my castle?" Oren demanded as his guards' eyes fluttered open. Oren was furious. He was lost as to how anyone could let Heliodor back into his castle, let alone take Willow from his protection. This was his castle, a place that was supposed to be safe and protected against unwanted visitors.

"I expect immediate answers. My family's lives may very well have been in danger, and you morons let someone knock you unconscious and slip by?" Oren continued.

Only one member of the royal guards dared to step forward and answer the Dark Fae king. "Adair told us that we didn't have to worry about any intrusions because you enchanted the castle against people that you have not allowed in," he explained.

The Dark Fae king stared incredulously at the guard who had spoken, very much unimpressed by the response he had received. His mask of calmness now broken; he unleashed his fury.

"First and foremost, Adair is no longer captain of the guard! You are supposed to get your orders from me! And secondly, surely you idiots must realize that if someone were to purposefully let someone in, the enchantments in the castle would fail!" The Dark Fae king's expression was that of anger, his fists clenched and shaking with rage.

After his outburst, not even one of his guards was willing to come forward and accept responsibility for their irresponsible actions. "You're all equally responsible and accountable for your own actions. For now, go back to your positions. I'll deal with every single one of you later." His unnamed threat hung in the air, and the guards trembled as they left the Dark Fae king alone in his throne room.

Going back to Willow's room, the Dark Fae king smelled the nightshade in the air, leading him to believe that Willow had been subjected to the same spell as his guards. Traces of golden sparkles were all over the walls, indicating that another spell had been used, perhaps to soundproof the room. The small dagger that she had been using was left on the floor, a grave reminder that the young woman hadn't intended on going down without a fight. The sun began rising through the window, which hung open, the golden morning rays indicating the start of a new day, but the storm inside Oren had just begun to brew. How dare that low-down, disgusting Light Fae kidnap his friend right from his castle. He was going to get her back, even if he had to destroy Heliodor himself.

For now, he went to wake Nerida. No doubt she was already awake after hearing all the noise that he made. She would be equally furious when she found out exactly what had transpired during the early morning hours.

CHAPTER 7

Darkness turned to light as Willow's eyes fluttered open, adjusting to the blindingly bright lights. She found herself in an unfamiliar room. The chandelier was shaped into flowers that she had never seen before. The room was filled with many gold and light-colored flower decorations; the color scheme and patterns on the blanket were the same.

She got out of bed and made her way over to the door, grasping the handle and attempting to open the door to no avail. Windows lined the other side of the room, but when Willow approached them, her view was obstructed by thick metal bars. No doubt they were meant to prevent her escape. Glancing out through the bars, she could only make out the tops of a few withered tree branches.

Before Willow could further contemplate what to do next, the door opened and in walked Heliodor, flanked by two guards who wordlessly grabbed Willow without giving her a chance to protest. They marched her down a series of dimly lit hallways that all but looked the same to the young woman. They stopped in front of an archway that had no doors and dragged her inside. There, in all her malicious glory, sat Nessa on her throne, her crimson-and-gold eyes staring intensely at the young woman in front of her.

"Queen Nessa, I have brought the Faeling from Oren's court as per your orders," Heliodor said.

"I don't know why you haven't dismissed yourself along with the guards, Heliodor. I want to speak to Willow alone, without any interruption," Nessa said with an icy tone.

She continued to ignore the Light Fae as he bowed and left the room. "I suppose you're wondering why I've brought you here, though judging by your expression, you've already figured it out." Willow crossed her arms and remained silent.

The Dwarf queen chuckled. "I can assure you that I have no intentions of harming you, despite what that idiot Heliodor said. But if you prefer to stay silent, then I have no qualms," Nessa continued.

Willow decided that either way, she was stuck in an unknown place with an enemy, but she would engage as little as possible, not because she feared what the Dwarf queen could possibly do to her, but because she didn't want to waste her time talking to someone who had very obviously lost all sense.

"If that was so true, then he wouldn't have me brought here on your orders. You could have just extended an invitation to me," Willow said with a neutral expression, not wanting to give any part of her thoughts or fears away.

Nessa chuckled. She knew that Willow's power was wild from

years of disuse. From what the bumbling fool Heliodor told her, if Willow had practice, she could destroy a whole kingdom and then some.

"Perhaps you're right, but maybe you wouldn't have accepted my invitation. After all, the Dark Fae king must have already poisoned your mind about the Light Alliance."

Willow wasn't going to fall for Nessa's mind games. Anyone in their right mind could see that she was trying to manipulate the young woman. "You can say what you'd like about Oren, but you are one hundred percent wrong. Nothing you say about him will ever convince me to come over to your side. He didn't have to tell me anything about you or your alliance."

Nessa let out a maddening laugh, a clear indication to the young woman that she was not in her right mind. "It's clear to me that you, dear Willow, have no idea how much power and influence Oren has over you, and you're clearly not in the right state of mind. If you joined my alliance, then you would see the light. That despicable Dark Fae is tainting you with his darkness. He's only using you for your incredible power. He even calls himself the high king. How arrogant it is for someone like him to flaunt his powers like that? He has even sought to destroy the Light Fae, and this war is just an excuse to rid the realm of them. I even sent Heliodor to reason with him, but what does he do? Makes you attack Heliodor to provoke him and then decides to throw him the dungeon!"

Willow's face remained unchanged. "First of all, you had me kidnapped and brought over here just to convince me that Oren is evil, and you expect me to listen to all the false claims that you've been spewing from your mouth for the past ten minutes. You think that just because Oren is a Dark Fae, he's automatically considered evil? Where's the logic in that? I have not heard a single thing that you've done to prevent this conflict between the courts. Why is your Alliance even called the Light Alliance to begin with? It's obvious to me that you're the one pulling all the strings," Willow said. She paused a moment to catch her breath, ensuring she didn't lose control—it could mean life or death in this situation. "And all I've heard from you about Oren is that he is evil and that he's been plotting this from the very start. You sent Heliodor to his castle so that he would kill Oren, I wouldn't call that a successful peace talk."

SLAP!

The sound of Nessa's palm hitting Willow's cheek echoed throughout the room, the mark of five fingers appeared, bruising her cheek. And though Nessa's slap left a searing pain on her cheek, Willow did not flinch, let alone shed a single tear. Nessa seethed in anger at this, her face red and her body fuming with anger at the fact that Willow would not be swayed by her words and reasoning, nor by her physical abuse.

"How dare you presume to tell me that Oren isn't evil! He's very obviously tainted your mind with stories about how evil the Light Fae are! Can you not see how powerful you really are? Your powers are unlike anything anyone has seen in ages, and you want to waste your time with the Dark Fae Court when you could be training and learning to hone your powers with some of the most powerful leaders in the Light Alliance?"

Willow was unfazed by the Dwarf queen's slap and temper,

COURT OF THE DARK FAE

giving her a simple answer. "Not everything dark is evil, just like not everything light is good. Oren hasn't attacked anyone the way you have. You literally sent Heliodor to attack Oren whilst he was in my hometown and again in his own castle. How do you expect him to react? By sitting down and acting as if nothing happened? It seems odd that you claim Oren is evil when all you've done is sent Heliodor to kill him, and over a position of leadership no less. I have not seen a single ounce of arrogance coming from him. As a matter of fact, you seem to be the arrogant one, thinking that you deserve to be the high queen." Willow looked Nessa right in the eye. "To top it all off, you claim to be so good, but you clearly aren't. The slap you just gave me is a good indication of that. I'm no fool, and you shouldn't have taken me for one either."

Nessa was taken aback by Willow's fierceness. She thought that even though she had unexpectedly struck the young woman, that would have at least reduced her to tears on the floor.

"I'd say you are the fool for ignoring my offers and being blind to the fact that you've been brainwashed by the Dark Fae king! You've only just met him, and yet you already give your full trust to a mad Fae like him?"

Willow scoffed. "That's rich, especially coming from you. I've only just met you as well, and you've already managed to make yourself look like a villain. You didn't even need Oren's help doing that, seeing as how you managed to have Heliodor kidnap me on your orders. That in itself makes you the evil one."

SLAP!

Nessa struck Willow's other cheek. Willow stood still and

unmoving. The silence was suffocating, the Dwarf queen having nothing else to say to the defiant young woman in front of her. After several moments, Willow continued.

"I hope you're having fun proving yourself to be the villain. Because if you were trying to show that there's one enormous difference between you and Oren, you've done a great job."

Having no proper response for her, Nessa summoned the two guards with a snap of her fingers. Immediately, the two silent guards that had dragged Willow appeared behind her once more; no doubt they would drag her back to the same room.

"Take Willow back to her room. I'm sure once had the chance to reconsider her options, she will be more open-minded to our conversation."

The guards gripped Willow's wrists a bit more harshly than they had when they initially brought her to Nessa's throne room, bruising them in the process. They dragged her back to her room and threw her on the floor. They slammed the door and clicked the lock into place it before storming off, leaving Willow to pick herself up off the ground.

If Nessa thought that holding Willow prisoner would get her to side with Light Alliance, then she was sadly mistaken. The only problem Willow was facing at the moment was the fact that the room she was being held in was on an upper floor and the windows were covered in thick iron bars.

The door suddenly opened, hitting the wall with such force that Willow was startled out of her thoughts.

"You have some nerve talking to Queen Nessa like that, Faeling!" yelled Heliodor. "You should consider yourself

COURT OF THE DARK FAE

lucky she didn't have you thrown into the dungeons for your insolence!"

Willow was not in the mood to deal with Heliodor, so she crossed her arms and stayed silent.

Taking that as a sign of defiance, the Light Fae grabbed her arms and shoved her into the wall before she could even blink. Willow swallowed a whimper that was creeping up her throat.

She refused to let the Light Fae know that he possibly bruised her back from the shove.

"You must really be out of your mind if you think that acting tough is going to save you. Perhaps you are a Faeling, but you are not as powerful as you think. That little stunt you pulled in Oren's palace was nothing!" He pushed her body harder into the wall from behind. Willow remained silent.

"I suppose you think this false sense of bravado will get me to leave, but you are wrong. You're quite lucky that Nessa only struck you instead of throwing you in the dungeons to be tortured! Maybe when she calls for you in the morning, you'll finally gather some sense in your mind!"

Seeing that he wasn't going to elicit a response from the Faeling, Heliodor pushed her to the floor and left, slamming the door behind him. When she was sure that the Light Fae would not be able to hear her, Willow finally cried out in pain from all the trauma that she had received whilst being in Nessa's kingdom for less than a few hours. A few tears escaped from her eyes, falling down her cheeks like watery pearls. After collecting herself, Willow gathered her resolve—she knew she had to focus on escaping before she had more than bruises.

CHAPTER 8

Lightning flashed across the sky, and the sounds of thunder echoed across the Dark Fae Court, a heavy indication that a storm was brewing, representing exactly what the Dark Fae king was feeling. He was furious that Heliodor had managed to not only escape the dungeons but also sneak back into his castle and kidnap Willow.

He sat silently in his throne room, contemplating how he would rescue Willow. He was quite certain that she was in Nessa's kingdom, because where else would the idiotic Light Fae take her? His thoughts were interrupted by the sound of a knock.

"Who is it?" Oren asked, masking his irritable mood as best as he could.

"Lady Anthea, your highness. I have with me Lady Aislyn; she understands that you aren't in the mood to speak to anyone, but she would like to discuss an important matter with you."

Oren wasn't really in the mood to entertain his newest ally but nevertheless decided that if Lady Aislyn wanted to speak to him on an important matter, then he would listen.

"Very well, Lady Anthea, bring her in." Lady Aislyn walked into the room, right behind Lady Anthea, looking a bit concerned and irritated.

"I apologize for disturbing you, King Oren, but I have some news that I thought I should share with you. My mother, Queen Calista of the Shapeshifters, has joined Queen Nessa's alliance, and from what I have heard, they are plotting to infiltrate and disband your alliance, as well as Nessa's own plans to become high queen of the realm."

"Are you quite certain of this, Lady Aislyn?" Oren inquired.

It seemed odd to Oren that Lady Aislyn's mother would speak to her daughter about her plans, given that Lady Aislyn's mother knew she had joined Oren's alliance.

"I'm quite sure. I heard her myself. I sometimes visit my mother despite her and my father no longer being united, and I caught her speaking in her throne room with someone I hadn't seen before. I caught some of their conversation and found out that she's on Nessa's side. My mother is also responsible for the deadly nightshade mist that rendered most of your guards unconscious." She paused for a moment. "And she knows that Willow is being held prisoner in Nessa's castle."

Oren sat down to think on everything Lady Aislyn told him for a moment before his response.

"I had a hunch that Heliodor had taken Willow to Nessa's castle. I am not surprised that your mother jumped into an alliance with someone like Nessa. I know your mother to be quite impulsive," Oren said matter-of-factly.

"Is there anything I can do to assist you in rescuing Willow?" asked Lady Aislyn. It was clear she was feeling a bit guilty that the young woman was being held prisoner and that her mother was partially responsible for it.

"I don't think that I require any assistance for now. Should I have a need, then I will send a message to your court," Oren shared.

"I'll go now then; I deeply apologize for intruding so late," she replied.

"You didn't intrude. You've provided some helpful information. Perhaps you should stay for the night. I can see plainly that a storm is brewing, and I wouldn't want you to get stuck in the middle of it." The Dark Fae king felt it would only be fair to let the young Dragon Changeling stay after she had come all this way in stormy weather.

"I appreciate the kind offer, your majesty, but I can just teleport myself back to my father's castle," she answered.

"Safe travels then, Lady Aislyn." As soon as the Dark Fae king bid her farewell, Lady Aislyn disappeared in a flurry of silver flames. Before he could say anything to Lady Anthea, she had already sensed that the king wanted to be left alone, so she bowed and left the throne room.

Minutes after Lady Anthea and Lady Aislyn left, Prince Lyndell came barreling in, the Dark Fae king once again being interrupted from his thoughts.

"Did you find Willow yet? Is she alright? Are you going to rescue her?" Lyndell sputtered out quickly.

Oren glared at Lyndell because of the manner in which he

had entered the room. "Why do you insist on making a scene, Red? Can you not see that I am in no mood to socialize, least of all with you?" Words could not describe the annoyance the Dark Fae king was feeling toward Lyndell in that exact moment.

"I came by to see if I could help!" Lyndell tried and failed to explain to his friend who looked like he really wanted to murder Lyndell.

"You're not helping! You are being more of a nuisance at this moment!" Oren shouted. Before the Dark Fae king could say anything else, Nerida came through the doors of the throne room.

"Oren, darling, you've not eaten anything all day. I think it would do you some good to eat something. I've even made your favorite blue pumpkin soup," Nerida stated in obvious concern. She knew he was upset, but she also knew that it wouldn't do Willow any good if he was in poor health when he came to her rescue.

He sighed. "Very well, dear. If you insist that I eat something, then I will." He stood up from his throne and walked out of the room toward the dining hall.

"That's all it took to get him to leave? I've been trying to annoy him for ages and all he did was stare at me with his death face!" Lyndell blurted all this out after Oren had left to not further incite his fury. Nerida chuckled at Lyndell's statement. "You better not say that around him; he might actually be tempted to throw you out in the storm."

"I can handle his temper. He's not that scary," Lyndell said. As soon as those words left his mouth, Oren came back into the room.

"Oh? So, you don't think I'm scary," Oren said with a flat mouth. Lyndell screamed and jumped a considerable height into the air upon hearing Oren's voice. Oren rolled his eyes at his friend's antics and turned to Nerida, holding out his arm. "Shall we go and eat, dear?"

She laughed and took his arm. "Of course. Lyndell, you're welcome to join us."

"Wouldn't it be easier to toss him outside in the storm?" asked Oren.

Nerida lightly smacked his arm. "Come on, darling, he's your friend. You wouldn't want him to get sick from being wet and cold."

Oren sighed in exasperation. "Oh, alright. You'd better hurry up and get off the floor if you want something to eat, Red."

The three of them left the throne room for the dining hall, sitting down at the large table and eating the blue pumpkin soup that Nerida had made.

"I have to devise a plan to free Willow from Nessa and Heliodor's clutches," Oren said as they were sitting around the table after the meal, drinking a sparkling blue tea that smelled like rhododendron flowers.

"Isn't it a bit risky to leave the castle unprotected while you go and rescue Willow? And don't forget, you still haven't done anything to Adair for being a traitor!" Lyndell was a bit concerned that his friend wasn't thinking things through and that he was leaving Nerida and Wisp unprotected.

"And you call me the dramatic one. Have you forgotten that the castle is embedded with my most powerful spells? Not to mention that Nerida has powerful magic as well. She is also more than capable of taking care of herself, should the need to fight ever arise and I'm not here. As for that traitor, Sir Ash is keeping a close eye on him. When the time is right, I will make sure he pays dearly for betraying me and my court!" Oren explained to his friend in utter exasperation while glaring at him from the corner of his eye.

"Alright, no need to get so angry," Lyndell replied sheepishly, even though he was the one that initiated the conversation in the first place.

"He's only irritated that Nessa has Willow in her clutches and with good reason, too. She will most definitely try to convince Willow to ally with her Light Alliance and that Oren is evil," Nerida said, trying to calm Oren and Lyndell down, though admittedly, she was worried about Willow as well. No one knew whether she had decided to ally herself with Nessa or not. After all, the Dwarf queen was one of the most manipulative beings in the realm.

"Worry not, Nerida, I will rescue Willow and Nessa will regret ever taking her." With that declaration, Oren left the table, quite obviously to plan Willow's rescue. Throwing open the doors to his throne room, Oren surrounded himself with as many maps and books of the Light Fae Kingdom as he could. Hopefully, he would be able to find a way to bring Willow back safely.

CHAPTER 9

Night fell in Nessa's kingdom rather quickly. The stars littered and glittered like a thousand gemstones against the black sky. It seemed that everyone in the castle aside from the guards, Nessa, and Heliodor were soundly sleeping. Willow stared outside of the tower window, contemplating how she could escape from Nessa's castle. It was very likely that Oren knew she had been kidnapped, but she didn't want the Dark Fae king to risk everything just to come to her rescue.

Who knew how long it would be before Nessa lost her patience with Willow and threw her in the dungeons; a place like that would be much harder to escape from. She was unable to use her powers properly. They had manifested when she needed them the most back when Heliodor first attacked the Dark Fae Court. Now, she couldn't even summon a single spark within her fingertips.

Muffled voices sounded outside of her door, snapping Willow out of her stargazing reverie.

She ran across the room and pressed her ear against it.

"You idiot! You told me that she would be willing to join our side! How dare you bring me that insolent brat!" Nessa seethed.

"Well, how was I to know, Queen Nessa? It's not as though I can read her into her emotions! How was I to know that she would be so uncivil toward you?" said Heliodor.

Nessa scoffed at Heliodor's stupidity. "Given the fact that she managed to subdue you should have been the biggest clue!"

"Oh, please, Queen Nessa, one fluke does not make an entire personality!"

"Does it not, Heliodor? It shows that she was willing to risk her life to protect someone she hardly even knew! If that's not the most self-righteous thing an individual can do, then you clearly have no idea of the definition of compliant!" she screamed.

"You standing here arguing about her isn't helping us get rid of the Dark Fae king, Queen Nessa!"

Amidst their arguing, a third muffled voice interrupted.

"Your majesty, General Heliodor, the Dark Fae Adair has some information he obtained while perusing the Dark Fae king's library. Being a Faeling doesn't necessarily mean you have half the magic of your Fae parent. It just means that you are limited with how you can use it. As you are well aware, a Faeling has to have an object, such as a wand or a spell book, in order to channel their magic. And of course, Faelings do not possess wings, unlike normal Fae.

"The reason why she is more powerful than a normal Faeling was unfortunately the only piece of information that I was not able to glean from Adair," finished the messenger. Nessa digested the information for a moment.

"You can bring as much information about Faelings as you want, Heliodor. If she does not comply with my demands, then I will see to it that you have no place in my court or alliance," Nessa finished with finality as her footsteps indicated that she had walked away.

The new information sunk in Willow's head like a heavy piece of metal. Willow was not the person she thought she was. She glanced at her hands and clenched them into fists, shaking with a mix of emotions. She hadn't been anyone special until she met Oren and saved his life. Being thrust into a role that she did not want made her feel sick.

She fell back against the door, head in her hands, and thought of ways she could escape. Willow knew that the risk of using her powers was great; after all, the first time that she had used them had drained her of strength. Gathering her resolve, she stood up, gripped the cold metal bars on the window, and closed her eyes, focusing all her power into the bars. She could feel the tingling sensation of the magic rushing through her blood and into her fingertips. A minute passed, and she heard a slight hissing sound. She cracked her eyes open; metal was dripping on the floor in silver rivulets. The melted metal made a silver pool around her feet, and her view through the window was no longer obstructed. She did it. Willow felt as if the weight on her heart was lifted at the manifestation of her powers. She felt shocked and elated that her plan had worked.

Willow stuck her head out of the hole, stealing a glance toward the treetops. Glancing down, she saw a cluster of ivy growing alongside the outer wall of the tower. Leaning slightly out of the window, she concentrated the remainder of her magic and strength into growing the plant a little closer to the window.

Willow was starting to feel the effects of having used so much of her energy at once; nevertheless, she persevered. Exhaustion was better than being imprisoned in a strange place by individuals who were trying and failing to prove that Oren was an evil Fae and that he would rain destruction upon everyone in the realm. Eventually, the vine made its way to just outside her window.

Gripping the plant like it was a ladder, she made her descent, finally standing firmly on the ground. Not having much of a choice, she made her way into the dense forest nearby. Willow knew that she would have a better chance of hiding out there than staying visible. The moon shone brightly overhead, illuminating the path to the forest as Willow silently made her way in. Despite being in pain, she walked for what seemed like an eternity before stumbling upon a curtain of vines that concealed a hidden waterfall. Thousands of gems were embedded in the rocks, sparkling myriad colors in the moonlight and creating an ethereal glow.

As Willow walked around the hidden waterfall, a pink orb of light circled round her head and vanished behind the waterfall. Curious as to where the light disappeared to, Willow walked up to the waterfall and saw a hidden cave behind the flowing water. She walked inside, and the bright gemstones sparkled, lighting the cave in the same myriad colors as the rocks outside.

"Welcome, Willow," an ethereal voice said.

"Who are you? And how do you know my name?" Willow

was afraid that she had been found by the guards of Nessa's castle and that she would be stuck inside the tower once more. She was beyond exhausted from the use of her powers, but the fear of getting captured once more outweighed any fatigue that she had. Instead of speaking, the voice that welcomed Willow revealed herself as a figure glowing in a white light. Dark, coal-colored hair with streaks of dark pink sat in an elaborate bun with a crown of braids on top of the figure's head. A few pink cherry blossoms were placed alongside the braids, almost like a secondary crown made up of flowers. Rather than wearing clothes, it appeared as if the figure was wearing thousands of sparkling stars in the shape of a gown and bracelets made from blossoms adorned her wrists. Finally, after what seemed like an eternity, the glowing figure spoke in a voice that was as light as the breeze.

"My name is Azura. I'm the guardian of Elrein. That is what this cavern and the area of the forest surrounding this place is called. You are Willow Blackplum, daughter of Rowan and Florian Blackplum. Everyone believes that you are a Faeling because your powers are quite rare and feel much more powerful than that of normal Faeling. You have also just escaped the tower in which Nessa had been keeping you prisoner."

Willow felt uneasy after hearing Azura read her as though she was some book. "How did you know about my family? Have you been spying on them? Are you also in league with Nessa?" Willow prepared herself for the worst possible scenario, if it did indeed turn out that Azura was in league with Nessa, then she would fight her with any remaining strength that she had left.

"I know every single family in this realm, including those who left to live in the human realm. And it's certainly no secret that you could be the last Faeling. Although, your powers are quite curious. As for being in league with Nessa, I can assure you that I would not go so far as to ally myself with one so wicked, let alone one who is willing to start a war for the sake of being in power." Azura's statements quelled most of Willow's fears, including the fear that Azura was on Nessa's side.

"I can help you get back to Oren's kingdom, if that is what you wish. That is my specialty, after all," Azura said. She opened a glowing pink portal that showed a worried Oren sitting in his throne room amidst a pile of maps and books. "He's worried about you. I can't guarantee that my portal will land you directly outside his castle. He has enchantments that even I cannot break, no matter how powerful I may seem, but I can guarantee you that you will be transported back to his court."

Willow contemplated this information with a slightly wary expression, although Azura had a point. If Oren was powerful in his own right, then it would make sense that no one could appear inside his castle unless they had his permission or were able to create a shadow key. Azura saw Willow's apprehension and sensed that the young woman would not be easy to convince.

"I know that you must be feeling mistrustful, but I can assure you that I mean you no harm. If I wanted to take you back to Nessa, then I would not offer you a way back to the Dark Fae Court," Azura stated once more to Willow.

Willow sighed. "Alright. I trust you to send me back to Oren's court." Willow, being drained of energy and not having much strength to continue walking, didn't really have much of a choice here. At this point, anything was better than being stuck in Nessa's side of the realm.

Standing in front of the portal, Willow bid the guardian a farewell and stepped through. Instead of walking through the portal and appearing in Oren's throne room, she ended up on the front steps of his castle.

The two guards that happened to see Willow appear on the doorstep were Lady Anthea and Sir Ash—the two sibling knights who had been acquainted with her previously.

"Willow! You're here? But how?" asked Ash. Glancing at the bruises that were still prominent on the young woman's face, their expressions darkened.

"What in the realm? You're hurt!" screamed Anthea. Before Willow could respond properly, she pitched forward, exhaustion taking over and her world turning dark once more.

CHAPTER 10

As the young woman fell forward, Sir Ash acted quickly and caught her before she could hit the ground.

He carried her inside, closely followed by Lady Anthea.

"Go and tell his majesty that Willow has returned. I'll go and put her in one of the guest rooms lining the dragonfly wing," Sir Ash told his sister before he turned down the hall. He found an empty room and placed Willow on the bed. The room had the black enchanted dragonflies on the walls, as well as a similar wardrobe and vanity to her previous room. Ash pulled a blanket over her unconscious form, eyebrows creased with worry as he turned to the enchanted dragonflies.

"Watch over her. I'll be right back," he told the dragonflies.

"As you wish Sir Ash!" the dragonflies chattered all at once as he turned and left the room.

Lady Anthea sped in the opposite direction from the hall, determined to break the news to the Dark Fae king before he decided to set out to rescue the person who had ended up making it back.

In his throne room, Oren stood while studying a map of the other half of the realm, surrounded by plans and weapons as preparation to rescue Willow from Nessa's clutches. One thing was for certain, he would make Nessa and her allies pay dearly for not only trying to incite a war, but also taking Willow right from under his nose in his own court. Suddenly, the doors to his throne room burst open, and Lady Anthea came rushing in, breathless.

"Your majesty! Willow has returned but she's hurt! She lost consciousness, so Sir Ash had to carry her inside!" Lady Anthea said in a rush, so much so that the Dark Fae king could barely piece together a single syllable coming out of her mouth.

"Breathe and speak a little slowly, Lady Anthea. I can't understand a word of what you are saying. Or rather, what you are trying to say." The Dark Fae king was agitated that he had been interrupted, even more so now that Lady Anthea had just barged in and mashed together all of her sentences, making it near impossible for Oren to understand her.

Lady Anthea took a deep breathe. "Willow has returned. She showed up on the doorstep and then collapsed before we could say anything. She's been injured as well." The look on the Dark Fae king's face darkened upon hearing that Willow was hurt.

"Take me to her at once!" he screamed. Before Lady Anthea could open the door and lead the way, another individual came crashing into Oren's throne room, his red hair flying wildly in all directions and his crown askew. Falling to the floor with a thud, he looked up sheepishly at Oren's face, only to notice that instead of the usual mask of irritation that he specifically reserved for Lyndell, he looked like he was going to murder someone.

"I can see that I've come at a bad time . . . " Lyndell started, but before the Moon Elf prince could continue, Oren wordlessly stepped away from him and followed Lady Anthea outside.

"She's in the dragonfly wing of the castle your majesty." Lady Anthea had never seen her king look so angry, at least not to the point where he didn't even acknowledge Lyndell's presence.

"No doubt she is still unconscious. It must have taken her quite a bit of power to escape Nessa's clutches the way she did." Oren's brow creased with worry for his friend. After all, Willow's powers weren't like those of a normal Faeling; she had no proper control of them, and as such, they drained her energy.

Sir Ash walked inside Oren's throne room to collect a few papers when he tripped over something, or rather, someone.

"Hey! Watch it!" Ash said. He was annoyed that he had been tripped by an unknown person on the floor of the throne room.

"If you actually watched where you were walking, maybe you wouldn't have tripped over me! And it's rude to yell, you know!" Lyndell exclaimed.

"Oh! Your highness! I didn't realize I tripped over you, I'm so sorry!" Sir Ash panicked at the fact that he may have insulted Prince Lyndell. "My sincerest apologies, your highness," Sir Ash said as he bowed to the Moon Elf prince.

"I mean, I don't know if I feel like forgiving you. You yelled at me, after all." Hearing Lyndell say that drained the color from Sir Ash's face and made Lyndell burst out laughing.

"I'm only joking, Sir Ash! No need to look like you've already been sentenced to the dungeons!" Lyndell continued, laughing so much that he needed to stop for air.

"Your highness, maybe you should go back home. No one's in the mood for jokes," Sir Ash looked at him, unimpressed.

"Lighten up, Sir Ash, and I've told you before, you can call me Lyndell!" he finished with a small laugh, although Sir Ash's face showed no traces of amusement. "Oh alright. I'll go back home. But I do have a message for Oren. Tell him the moon is full."

"What do you mean by that, your highness?" asked Sir Ash in confusion.

Much to his chagrin, instead of answering him, the redheaded Moon Elf prince quickly stood up and smiled, before rushing off and leaving an agitated Sir Ash standing in the throne room.

In the shadows, a figure had been standing, undetected by either Sir Ash or Prince Lyndell.

Having heard what the two had been talking about, the figure vanished into the shadows.

Swiftly, the Dark Fae king walked toward the dragonfly wing of the castle. When he reached Willow's room, he softly opened the door. He dismissed Lady Anthea who bowed and left to attend to other duties.

The expression on his face darkened upon seeing Willow's bruised and battered state. With a quick glance, he could see that she looked pale, almost as if all color had been drained from her. Much to his anger, he saw the bruises on both of her cheeks, as well as the ones that littered her wrists. He felt her pulse, and much to his shock, it was almost nonexistent. Summoning a powerful spell that crackled with purple energy, he held Willow's hand and restored some of the energy she had used up.

Almost immediately, some color returned to her cheeks, and her pulse became steady once more. After that was done, he waved a hand over her body, a beam of silver burst from his fingertips, healing all wounds, whether they had been visible to him or not. Despite his best efforts to replenish the energy that had been lost, she did not awaken. This meant that she would need to rest in order to recover.

Before he left, Oren cast a spell over the entire room, ensuring that no one would be able to enter the room without his permission, keeping Willow safe should the Light Fae, or anyone else for that matter, attempt to kidnap her again. After that was done, Oren turned and left hoping that Willow would pull through. As soon as he walked out into the hall, he collided with Nerida. "Oh! I'm sorry, Oren, darling. I just heard from Lady Anthea that Willow escaped. Is she alright?"

Oren sighed. "Don't fret, Nerida. She's fine now. I've healed her wounds; all she needs now is proper rest." A dark look passed over Nerida's face when she heard that Willow had been hurt.

"She was hurt? By whom?" Nerida hardly ever showed her anger, but upon hearing that Willow had gotten injured, anger suddenly rose.

"I suspect that Nessa and Heliodor are responsible. Who else would be stupid enough to put their hands on her?" Oren replied.

Nerida's face was unchanging, but inside, a storm of anger was definitely brewing. "When we finally face the Light Alliance, Nessa is mine. She's going to pay for what she did to Willow," Nerida said with resolve.

"Believe me, Nerida, the whole entirety of Nessa's alliance is going to pay for their actions. They seek to destroy me and that's fine. However, involving the individuals whom I care about is another low, and I will make every single responsible party pay for their deeds!" Both Oren and Nerida turned and left the dragonfly wing to prepare for a possible war—a war they both knew was most likely unavoidable.

CHAPTER 11

Lightning crackled and thunder shook the realm, at least the part of the realm that Nessa dwelled in—though the Dwarf queen had nothing to with the weather on the outside.

She, however, was in perfect control of the situation in front of her. The sounds of screaming and multiple objects being thrown about in the room could be heard from within the already dark and dismal castle, all swirling together in a loud symphony of chaos.

"How could you let her escape, Heliodor? Do you have any idea what you've done? If I had my way with the girl, then I could have had another powerful ally by my side! She would have been our greatest weapon! Her powers are unlike anything I've ever sensed before! You had one simple task that even an idiot could understand! How did she escape?" she demanded. The Dwarf queen's crimson-and-gold-colored eyes were filled rage as she spoke and stared down at the Light Fae kneeling down in front of her, the rings on her fingers crackling with white lightning.

"You have my deepest apologies, Queen Nessa. I was not aware that the girl was able to use her powers to escape." Heliodor trembled ever so slightly as he bowed to Nessa. He knew he had ruined things for the Light Alliance by being arrogant and not keeping any guards posted outside of the wretched girl's room. He hadn't anticipated that Willow would escape and that had been a fatal mistake on his part.

The Dwarf queen dangerously narrowed her eyes, and promptly struck Heliodor with the full force of the lighting energy absorbed by her rings. Being that he was already on the ground, it didn't take much force for the kneeling Light Fae to crumple and fall unconscious, though Nessa did not take notice of this yet.

"You cost me an advantage over Oren, and all you can do is pathetically sit there and apologize to me? How dare you think your pitiful excuses would grant you any mercy! Did you not consider that despite being untrained in using her powers, she would find a way to escape regardless? You did not think those things through, and you had the audacity to tell me that you would personally make sure that she would stay imprisoned in the tower! Now I must withdraw the call for the meeting with my alliance because I don't actually have the girl as my prisoner! I would have looked like a fool in the meeting saying I had a weapon when, in fact, I don't!" Nessa seethed. The walls of her castle shook with fury. Heliodor had proved to be a useless Fae, given that he had underestimated the girl and allowed her to escape.

Unfortunately for Nessa, she noticed that Heliodor had passed out from the pain during her tirade, so he had not heard a single word coming out of her enraged mouth after he had been attacked by the lightning. Seeing that the Light Fae wouldn't be conscious any time soon, Nessa turned and left the room, letting him lay on the ground. Turning the corner of the dimly lit hallway, she saw Adair approaching. As soon as he was face-to-face with the Dwarf queen, he bowed.

"Greetings, Queen Nessa. I trust you already know of the girl's escape," Adair spoke in a honeyed tone, hoping to appease the visibly angered Nessa.

"Yes, Adair. I'm well aware that the Faeling has escaped. Tell me something I don't already know."

Adair chuckled. "Were you aware that the prince of the Moon Elves has been gathering an army?"

Nessa's anger did not dissipate upon hearing Adair speak. If anything, her levels of anger were very visibly increasing. Her face twisted into an angry scowl, her eyes burning with the flame of anger.

"Prince Lyndell is gathering an army, and you're just now telling me this? What were you waiting for? There is no point in being an informant for me if you aren't going to deliver information on time, you wilted leaf!"

Adair responded calmly; he wasn't going to start a back-and-forth argument with the Dwarf queen. If she wanted to do that so badly, then she had Heliodor for that. "I came from Oren's court to yours specifically to deliver the news. I don't know if this has escaped your notice, but he clearly knows something is going on. I had to be very careful when I left. I did not come here to incite a childish argument, nor did I come here to call you names, Queen Nessa. You can argue with that moron Heliodor if you are itching for a fight."

"If there's nothing else, you're dismissed!" Nessa ignored Adair's jab at her in favor of dismissing the traitorous Fae.

"Very well. I will keep a close eye on any new developments and inform you if the situation changes." With a slightly irritated flutter of his violet wings, Adair left Nessa alone to her thoughts. Why Oren decided to keep the traitor in his midst was no mystery to Nessa. He was most likely keeping a close eye on the Fae. Nessa wondered how Adair kept the façade of a loyal guard when he knew that Oren had no trust in him. Perhaps the Dark Fae king was a fool after all and thought that demoting Adair's status would make him loyal. Regardless of the reason, one thing was certain: when the time came, she would destroy Oren using Willow's power. Whether or not she would agree was a different factor in Nessa's twisted story.

Night passed and morning came, though Willow had not yet awoken, not even stirring as the Dark Fae king came to see her. Feeling her pulse, he was relieved to find that it wasn't as weak as it had initially been. Oren blamed himself for the state that Willow was in. After all, he felt responsible for her well-being, and it was due to his carelessness about Adair that Willow had even gotten kidnapped and hurt in the first place. As he turned to leave the room once more, he heard Willow's voice call out softly.

"Oren?" At that instant, instead of turning to leave, the Dark Fae king walked back to the young woman's side.

"Are you alright, my dear?" he asked.

She blinked her eyes tiredly. "I'm fine, maybe just a little disoriented. The last thing I remember is appearing outside on the steps of your castle and nothing after that. How long have I been unconscious?" she asked.

"You were unconscious for the entirety of the day. And I suspect it was because you excessively used your powers whilst trying escape from Nessa's clutches and exhausted your magical core. Not to mention the fact that they dared to lay hands on you!" Oren had blamed himself for not acting quick enough to rescue her when she returned as weak as she did, almost upon death's door.

"It wasn't your fault that Nessa had Heliodor kidnap and imprison me," Willow began. "And it's also not your fault that I used my powers to escape; I was fully aware that it was a dangerous thing for me to do. But I would rather risk using them then becoming someone's pawn in a stupid game of power just to hurt you. And as for me getting hurt, I would take that over letting Nessa or Heliodor gain any sort of power over you." Willow spoke with sincerity evident in her voice. Willow hadn't known Oren for very long, but she would rather have been hurt a thousand times over if it meant keeping him safe.

The Dark Fae king was touched by her words, even more so because her actions reflected the sincerity in them. "I don't know how to thank you, my dear. It still doesn't ease my troubles knowing that they harmed you like that. I'll leave you to rest, and if you need anything at all, simply tell the dragonflies on the wall. They'll alert me and I'll come straight away."

Before he could say anything else, Willow fell unconscious once more. Oren softly closed the door to her room and made his way toward his secret room, where plans to destroy Nessa and her alliance were being made by none other than the Dark Fae king himself. One thing was certain in those plans: he would make Nessa and Heliodor feel pain a thousand times worse than what they inflicted on Willow.

CHAPTER 12

A literal and metaphorical storm was brewing once more in the realm as rain fell in a heavy torrent. Purple lightning flashed across the skies while the deafening roar of thunder drowned out any other noises. The inhabitants of Oren's castle all lay asleep, sans the guards who rotated every two hours under strict orders from their king. The traitorous Adair had not been included in the guard's rotations. Instead, he was sent home for the night. Scowling at the fact that his plans had been foiled, he left for Nessa's castle. The Dwarf queen was sitting on her throne when he arrived.

"What have you come for this time, Adair? Unless you've brought me the girl, I don't want to see you here," she stated tersely.

"Unfortunately for the both of us, the circumstances have changed. Oren has taken the liberty of not including me on the rotation of guards for this shift. And I cannot access the castle without an invitation due to the spell he has cast. Not even a shadow key would be of use," Adair retorted.

"You should have taken the girl before he had a chance to do that! What good is having a spy if you can't think on your feet? Get out of my sight and don't come back here unless you bring the girl!" Nessa yelled.

Scoffing, the Dark Fae left Nessa's castle and went off in a different direction.

Willow lay asleep as the storm raged on, tossing and turning, her dreamworld filled with tumultuous memories from a past that she could not be rid of so easily.

The sun shone as bright as a gem in the blue sky as fluffy white clouds floated softly. A man, a woman, and a young girl sat on the front porch of a house set back in the distance, each of them reading something to keep themselves occupied. Two younger children played around the yard whilst a younger Willow could be seen keeping a close eye on them. Suddenly, the sky darkened. Raindrops came down hard and fast, pelting those who were not underneath the shelter of the house. Running inside, the dark-haired family laughed at the bit of misfortune that happened to catch them in one of their peaceful moments.

The family sat around the table to enjoy their evening meal, all of them chattering happily.

Willow's smile was the brightest of them all.

"Mom! Dad! You'll never believe it, but Willow has been making all sorts of weird friends. I saw messages on her phone, and she's always sneaking off to hang out with them too. I would bet that she's also skipping classes to spend time with them. You guys think she's so good because she takes care of stuff around the house, but I think she's stupid and incompetent. Nothing about her character is good," a girl with dark hair and eyes taunted.

Quickly, the smiles that graced everyone's faces faded, replaced by looks of disgust and anger.

"You're no daughter of mine!" screamed a man with the same color hair and eyes as Willow.

"I knew you were trouble from the moment you were brought into this family. You're nothing but a burden of shame to this family!" the woman screamed.

"We should just kick you out! But even that would be too good for you. You'd just run off crying to your stupid little friends. I should make you drop out of school and get you fired from your job. Maybe then you'll understand that you can't do anything without my explicit permission!" the man threatened.

The things Willow was most afraid of in life had happened. Her sister, the one person whom she had thought would never do this to her, had spied on her and unfortunately gotten Willow into trouble.

She left for school the next morning; her mood ruined from the previous evening. Her friends, noticing her mood, tried to probe and pry her for an explanation.

"Come on, Will, there's something eating you . . . it's written all over your face," a pink-haired girl inquired with a sisterly tone.

A girl with icy-blue hair and black eyes elbowed her. "Can't you *see she's upset and doesn't want to talk right now, idiot?"*

"I am not an idiot!"

A small cough interrupted them. "She's gone," a girl with short, blonde hair and glasses said timidly. Willow had walked away from the table.

"I hope she's okay," a boy with long orange hair and soft brown eyes said.

Willow left the campus and went straight home before her friends could figure out what was wrong. They had been nothing but sweet and supportive to her, but she didn't want to burden them with the situation that she had been dealing with since the fallout with her parents.

Tears fell from her eyes as she stood in her bedroom, collecting things that were of importance. She made her decision. She placed a sealed envelope on the empty nightstand, and she walked out. Screams and curses were heard as she walked out in the hall, the voices not pausing to give her peace in the moment that she was leaving. Her friends never found out what had happened either, leaving the young woman with feelings of guilt and regret.

Willow shot up from the bed, gasping for air as the images from her dream burned into her mind. Her mind was muddled, not taking notice of the fact that she was not in her former home. She felt something take over her, as if she was not in control of the words leaving her mouth. Putting her hands over her ears, she spoke out in rushed sentences.

"I don't know why you believe her! Aerina, Dad, I didn't do anything like that! You have to believe me. I promise you it's not like that! Stop yelling, please!" Willow screamed.

Sensing that the young woman was in distress from the way she was speaking and breathing, the dragonflies immediately called the Dark Fae king to come. Oren appeared just moments later, his hair slightly ruffled from sleep. He walked toward Willow, who was still panicking and mumbling about her family. She was so distraught and distracted, she hadn't noticed Oren enter her room. He stopped and sat down in front of her, gently grasping her shoulders, his calm eyes staring into her panicked ones.

"Willow, focus on my voice. Take a deep breath, my dear. You are safe here, no one is going to raise their voice toward you, I promise," Oren said softly.

Finally shaking herself out of her stupor, she focused on Oren's calming voice, taking a deep breath and calming down enough to be able to speak coherently. "What happened?" she asked weakly, looking around the room and finally taking notice of her surroundings.

"I believe you had a nightmare, my dear. It would seem that from the words you were uttering that you were dreaming of your family."

"I'm sorry, I didn't mean to wake you," she apologized, looking guilty for bothering the Dark Fae king.

"You have nothing to apologize for, Willow. I came because I was concerned when the dragonflies alerted me that you were not breathing properly and that you spoke as if you were speaking to someone when there were no other figures present. I didn't come because it was inconvenient to me. I came because we're friends, and friends look after each other, not because you are being a burden to me." Those words from Oren warmed Willow's heart and eased some of the pain she felt from reliving a past memory.

"Thank you, Oren." Willow's greatest fear was being a burden to others. That was the main reason she slipped away from the friends she had made previously. And it was why she had left, after all, her mother told her as much. That was when Willow decided that enough was enough and she had taken the appropriate steps to get away and leave everything behind.

"You are most welcome. Do you think that you will be able to go back to sleep? You need to rest in order to regain your strength," said Oren.

Willow was hesitant to answer Oren's question; usually when she had a nightmare like that, it took her hours to feel safe enough to fall asleep again. The Dark Fae king noticed the hesitation but nonetheless let the young woman continue. "I might be able to go back to sleep in a few hours. I usually have a hard time going back to sleep when I have those nightmares."

Willow hoped Oren didn't think she was childish for not being able to sleep over a nightmare.

"Perhaps I can help with that my dear. Close your eyes and listen to my voice," Oren directed.

Willow settled back into bed and closed her eyes. Closing his own eyes for the moment, the Dark Fae king began reciting what sounded like a poem in a soft tone:

"Like a thousand stars that shine,
Silver dragonflies dance in the moonlight,
A gentle breeze blows through the meadow,

Filling the air with the sweet fragrance of rhododendrons,
Listen closely to the rushing of the stream,
Magic is in the air,
Painting a picture of serenity,
Forget troubles that cause you endless sorrows,
Let them burden you no longer,
And dream peacefully once more."

By the time Oren had finished reciting the poem, the young woman had fallen fast asleep once more, a look of peace and contentment evident on her face. A stark contrast to the panicked state she had been in a few minutes' prior. Glancing one more time to make sure that Willow was indeed fast asleep, the Dark Fae king silently stood up and left the room, gently closing the door behind him.

Oren made his way back to his own room where Nerida was quietly waiting for him.

"Is she alright, Oren?" Nerida was worried that the young woman was in danger, despite the increase of security measures in the castle.

"She's fine now. She had a vivid nightmare from what I gathered and was unaware even after she had awoken that it was not real," Oren explained.

Nerida sighed in relief though her forehead creased in worry for Willow. "Did you get Willow to go back to sleep?" she asked.

Oren nodded. "I actually used a dreamless sleep spell to help with that. She should be fully rested when she wakes up in the morning."

The worried look on Nerida's face left and was replaced by a yawn.

Noticing this, Oren took the blanket that was on the bed and covered the both of them with it, as sleep took a hold of them once more.

CHAPTER 13

While the inhabitants of one castle were somewhat peacefully sleeping, the inhabitants of another were plotting, seeking to destroy a king they all despised on the word of one queen.

Sitting around an ornate table in the dimly lit halls of Nessa's castle were none other than the leaders of her alliance.

"This would have been easier if you used essence of nightshade to poison the girl's mind. At least she would have been under our control," said a smooth yet cold voice belonging to the king of the Goblins.

"You are an idiot, King Nash. Essence of sun herb would be much better. At least this way we could control her without worrying about the effects wearing off," said Prince Sol.

"Watch your tone, Prince Sol. I am above you in so many ways. You are nothing but a lowly prince attempting to fill the boots of a king," the Goblin king responded.

The crackling of lightning was heard before Nessa's voice thundered in the room. "Silence! I grow tired of you idiots spouting useless ideas in my presence!"

King Nash scoffed. "If I may be so bold, Queen Nessa, while it may have been Heliodor who surprisingly captured the girl, the responsibility of keeping her here falls on your shoulders. She was being held on your orders in your own castle," shared Nash.

"Do keep going, Nash, with any luck, you might end up just like that moron Heliodor!" Prince Sol chuckled as he interrupted, having had no response to the Goblin king's prior insult.

"I'll have you know that I was the one who brought her here! If anyone did the most difficult part, it was me! How dare you imbeciles insult me!" Heliodor said furiously.

"Oh yes, I'm sure sticking her in a room with minimal security was so brilliant. Even a small child would be able to tell how idiotic that is!" Prince Sol said. He was getting fed up with Heliodor, never having liked the Light Fae to begin with. "At this point, it doesn't even matter who's fault it is—she's escaped and it's too late to think about what would have happened had Heliodor not been so lax with security."

"The fact of this entire matter is that we need to capture the girl and use her powers one way or another. We don't actually need her; we need her magic," stated the Shapeshifter queen.

"Ha! You say that, Queen Calista, but do you actually know anything about Faeling magic? They have to willingly let you use it, unlike normal magic, their magic is a fickle thing. If it does not recognize you as the master, then you have no hopes in using it for yourself," spouted Nash. King Nash was perhaps the most well informed on magic, thus the reason he was the most vocal.

Queen Calista turned her nose at the Goblin king, wishing she could refute his statement. Unfortunately for her, he was correct. Unless the Faeling willingly accepted, there was no way for her powers to be used against the Dark Fae king.

"You've forgotten something, King Nash. If Oren manages to take the Faeling under his tutelage, then we have no hopes in using her." All heads turned to see who had spoken, and where the cruel yet polite voice had even come from.

The cold voice belonged to Lord Obsidian, the leader of the Gnomes.

The dimly lit halls made his ink-black eyes and forest-colored hair even more intense, his gaze piercing each member of the alliance.

Gnomes were not known to be sociable individuals amongst the realm, and Lord Obsidian did not care much for the politics of the realm. He supposedly remained neutral until he was given a logical reason to attack Oren.

"Ah, Lord Obsidian. What a pleasant surprise. And here I thought you were on the side of the Dark Fae king." As per usual, Prince Sol could not keep himself from insulting others.

"Prince Sol, perhaps it would do you some good to actually study magic. It would make you sound a tad smarter than you look. And as I said in the meeting, I will not fight if not given reasonable points to do so." Lord Obsidian spoke carelessly, brushing imaginary dust off of his gold and black tunic.

"How dare you insult me, you plain little creature—" began Prince Sol.

CRASH!

The sound of a glass being thrown was heard throughout the

room before Prince Sol could continue his tirade against the Gnome lord.

"Shut up! All of you idiots seem to know so much about the girl's power and how to control her, yet none of you did anything when she was actually imprisoned!" Nessa's temper flared immensely as soon as the words left her mouth.

King Nash bit out, irritated that the alliance was being blamed for Nessa's incompetence. "You say we're the fools, but I believe you are the biggest fool of them all, Queen Nessa. Why don't you come up with an idea for your grand plan? You sit there getting angry with us for something that is actually your fault. Heliodor may be incompetent, but you are equal in that. He doesn't live in your court, which is where the Faeling was being held. Have you no common sense or did you perhaps fail in your study of magic as well? Every castle should have its own set of wards and spells, unique to the owner. I don't believe you did that, because had you done so, then the girl wouldn't have been able to escape. In your haste, you failed to realize that she is, indeed, very powerful. She is not just a simple human who used her power to subdue Heliodor. The young woman is quite intelligent, and she managed to escape without alerting a single guard in the vicinity of your castle. Before you start blaming us and pointing fingers, take a good look at who's castle she was in to begin with."

Speechless, Nessa could say nothing because the Goblin king was absolutely correct. If she hadn't been so boastful, then perhaps the Faeling would be standing here on the side of the Light Alliance.

"You're silent because he's right. If you hadn't wasted so much time getting angry with her, you would have convinced her to stay. Instead, you decided to strike her, not even once, but twice. Splendid job, by the way, convincing the girl that you weren't the villain," Lord Obsidian said. He was someone who didn't appreciate nonsense and thus spoke his mind, sounding polite with a hidden cruelness to his words.

"Honestly, what is the point of allying ourselves with someone who cannot take responsibility for their own actions? We're not children, most of us are rulers in different courts." A shockingly mature statement from the Sun Elf prince made the members of the Light Alliance raise their eyebrows, but since it was true, none of them decided to comment on it any further. "I say that each of us should try to capture the girl ourselves. At least one of us will keep a closer eye on her than Nessa ever did," Queen Calista said with a malicious glint in her eyes.

"You're speaking nonsense, Queen Calista. Don't you think the Dark Fae king is aware that there may be individuals who would try to infiltrate his court in order to get closer to the Faeling? How would anyone even get inside his castle?" Nash asked.

"As I'm sure you're aware, King Nash, I don't have to worry about that. I can change my appearance, after all," the Shapeshifter queen boasted to the Goblin king. She was the only one in her court who could also mimic the voice of the person she chose to shift into.

"You may have an advantage, but you forget, Oren is a master of magic. He didn't become the high king without merit and skills. And, unfortunately for you, he's exceptionally skilled in detecting deception. So, your plan to snatch the Faeling is very flawed," Nash responded.

Calista scoffed. "And you have a better plan, King Nash?"

A flash of lightning was visible through the windows; a loud crashing sound of thunder came into the hall right before Nessa slammed her hands on the ornate table, garnering everyone's attention once more.

"That's enough! Since you idiots are all so confident in your abilities, then I welcome you to try and capture the girl!" Nessa screamed.

"I think that's the most intelligent thing you've said all night, Queen Nessa. Our whole night was wasted arguing about your common sense. If I didn't know any better, I'd say you were trying to be the next high ruler after you get rid of Oren," speculated Obsidian. Having had enough, he stood up.

"Shut your mouth, you fool! I only seek to remove Oren so that we may get rid of his tyrannical rule. What kind of leader doesn't allow others to take the throne so that they may learn to be responsible in their own kingdoms? I brought this alliance together with the promise that we would all be equals. Make your baseless accusations elsewhere, Lord Obsidian!"

"And if I don't, what will you do to stop me, Queen Nessa? Let me remind you that I only came here for amusement. And if anyone must watch their tone, that would be you. Raising your voice toward me makes you sound very guilty." Lord Obsidian turned and left with a sweeping gesture and a not-so-subtle threat hanging in the air.

The remaining individuals in the room glanced in Nessa's direction, much to her irritation. "What are you idiots looking at me for? Go back to your courts! I've nothing else to say to any of you on this matter for now." In a flurry of skirts, Nessa quickly left Malachite Hall, leaving the remaining rulers to stare at one another before they too decided to travel back to their respective courts, not knowing what the next day would bring them.

"I see that Queen Nessa is once more running away from self-created problems," muttered Nash.

"Oh, shut up, Nash! I don't see you being any more helpful!" Heliodor retorted.

"I'm sorry, do you see me walking around like her faithful pet Heliodor? It honestly sickens me how the two of you have this grandiose plan to bring glory to the Light Alliance when you literally have no power to do so!" Nash spat.

Queen Calista rolled her eyes, "I think we should leave now. We can discuss this another time."

Before the Goblin king could retort, the rest of the disgruntled rulers left Malachite Hall to go back to their respective courts, leaving him with no other option but to leave as well, sneering at Heliodor and pushing him aside as he turned and left.

CHAPTER 14

While the night had ended up in troubles for nearly everyone, morning came swiftly. The golden rays of the sun finally peaked through the dark clouds that had previously been heralds to a storm.

Through the curtains of his bedroom, the sunlight shone onto Oren's face, effectively waking him up. Tossing aside his blankets, he stood up and got dressed for the oncoming day. He tossed on a black tunic embroidered with silver dragonflies and silver pants, carefully placing his pendant around his neck, as always.

Tugging on a pair of sapphire-colored boots, he brushed a hand through his ink-black locks and then stepped outside of his room, throwing open a set of glass doors that led onto a nearby balcony filled with silver chairs that held light blue cushions scattered with patterns of black dragonflies. There he stood, leaning on the elaborately carved railing, soaking in the sun's rays and letting the breeze ruffle his hair.

His pendant glistened in the morning light, as did his

mismatched sapphire blue eyes.

"How in the realm am I going to teach Willow to use her powers? I haven't encountered an individual like her before. And then there's the threat of the Dwarf queen. She thinks that being the high ruler is all about status. In reality, I have to make sure all the kingdoms are safe and well. Who do they think kept their subjects from facing starvation?" he said aloud to himself.

He sighed wistfully, the duties of being a high ruler were an enormous burden to shoulder.

The Dark Fae king paused in his musings when he heard light footsteps approaching. His mood ruined, he turned to berate the individual who had decided to come so close to him. However, his scowl softened upon seeing that the individual was Willow.

"Good morning, my dear. How are you? Did you sleep well?" Oren asked delicately, thinking of the rough night Willow had just had.

"Good morning, Oren. I'm fine. I slept well thanks to you. How are you?"

"I'm glad you were able to sleep well, my dear. I was just thinking about things. Mainly how Nessa is trying to wage a war and when I would be able teach you to use your powers without exhausting yourself to the point where you lose consciousness."

Willow let a sigh escape from her lips, an action that did not go unnoticed by the Dark Fae king.

"Is something troubling you, Willow?" he asked.

She looked thoughtful for a moment; she didn't want to bother the Dark Fae king with her problems. But she remembered him reminding her she wasn't a burden, and that she needed to start believing in that.

"I feel as though I brought extra troubles to your court when I arrived. Then there's the fact that I sort of woke you up just because of a few bad dreams."

Oren chuckled, if that's what Willow was worried about, then she really didn't have anything to be sorry for. "My dear, Nessa is a creature who thrives on chaos. She only seeks my position to gain the supposed power that I have. Never mind the fact that she is already a powerful queen of some of the fiercest creatures to dwell in her court. If she were to truly find out what it means to be the high ruler of the realm, then I can guarantee she would not be trying too hard to become one. Your presence only irritates her because you're an outlier in her otherwise flawless plan," Oren said softly.

"As for that nightmare you had, I take it that was not the first time you've had it. It seems to me that this is a rather common occurrence for you, a result of whatever conflicts you have had with your family. Regardless, it was no trouble at all, Willow. The poem you heard me recite to you was a spell to help you sleep. I do admit, I should have told you what I was going to do, but you were distressed, and I didn't wish to make you feel worse."

She shook her head and smiled; the both of them really were alike in some ways. "I just didn't expect Nessa would go that far. She's too consumed with trying to make you out to be a vile and wicked person. I suppose that's to be expected from someone like her. You are correct about the dreams. I have them almost every single night. They mainly stem from the way my younger sister treated me and how she manipulated my parents against me, which is what led to me leaving." She sighed wist-fully, remembering the happier times she had with her family, a look of melancholy appeared on her face.

Oren clenched his fists in hidden anger; it would probably be best if he didn't get visibly angry, lest he alert the whole castle that he was awake. "Your sister sounds exactly like Nessa. Why in the realm is your sister so antagonistic toward you, and why did your parents believe her? Of course, if you would prefer not to answer then that is fine, too."

Mulling over it for a minute, the young woman decided to tell Oren everything.

"It's a bit of a complicated and long story, if you have time, then I'll tell you what happened." He gently grabbed her hand—much to her embarrassment if her cheeks had anything to say about that—and pulled her toward the many chairs that littered the balcony.

"Let's sit down before you start telling me." After they had been seated, Willow began telling him her tale.

"As long as I can remember, my younger sister, Aerina, has manipulated me. Whether it was to clean her room or to do other things for her, I've done it all because she threatened me in some ways I hadn't thought were possible. If I so much as breathed a single word of what she was doing to my parents, then she told me that she would use evidence she had gathered against me to make them lose their faith and trust in me. She would spy on me, read through my letters and journals, take my things—anything a person could do to break down your trust in them and cross every bound-ary you have, she did it," Willow shared, pausing for a moment.

"She even came to me one day apologizing for acting immature, and I thought that was the end of it. I was very wrong because after that she was twice as rude and cruel to me; although since we were older, she did it in more subtle ways. One day, I was coming home from a break during college, and I came back to my sister looking at me with a smug face. She told me that since I decided to tell our parents how badly she'd been treating me, she was going to ruin the rest of my life," Willow said, looking off into the distance. "I ignored her because I didn't remember telling anyone anything, so she had to be bluffing. We had dinner as usual, and while I was talking, she interrupted, saying she had something important to tell my family. She then proceeded to tell them how cruel I had been to her over the years, repeating every single action she had done to me. In shock, all I could do was sit there and refute her claims but to no avail. They believed her over me, simply because I was the oldest and I should know better. She even told them I was lying about attending classes and hanging out with friends who were a bad influence. Then came the screaming and name calling. It was mainly my father and sister who did it. My mother tried to stop them when she could, but they didn't listen to her. I couldn't stand being called names or being screamed at every single day. So, I just left without so much as a proper goodbye. I didn't leave them any way to contact me or find me. It was also fairly easy for me to find a school in a new place, because I had excellent grades and they even offered to help me find a job. But after everything that happened, the nightmares just kept on coming. No matter what I try to do to forget the past, it seems to want to stick around."

At this point, the few tears that she had been trying to suppress escaped from the corner of her eyes, not escaping the notice of Oren who had been seething silently throughout the whole story. The Dark Fae king pulled the young woman into a hug, much to her surprise. Then he pulled out a handkerchief from the pocket of his shirt and dried the tears that were falling down her face.

"There's no need to waste your tears on individuals like them, my dear. In fact, I would like to see you smile instead. You have been through many conflicts in your life, but you did not let that change who you are. As for your sister, she seems like someone who is unsatisfied with her own life and decided to ruin yours for her own personal amusement," Oren shared.

Willow gave the Dark Fae king a watery smile. "I hope I didn't take too much of your time."

"Nonsense, my dear," Oren said while sitting up a bit straighter. "It was clear that you were upset. As for the dreams that plague you, I can give you a dreamless sleep until I think of a better solution. At most, you won't have any dreams, and there shouldn't be any side effects."

She thought for a quick moment; anything sounded better than seeing nightmares of her father and sister cursing her very existence.

"I wouldn't mind it. Anything is better than that."

Before the Dark Fae king could respond, shouts were heard within the courtyard. Swiftly standing up, the Dark Fae king grabbed Willow's hand once more and ran, quickly escorting her back to her room.

"Stay here, Willow. I shall return shortly."

The tone he used left no room for argument, so all she could do was nod her head and watch him leave before she closed the door and waited for him to come back.

CHAPTER 15

"Let go of me, you idiots! I haven't been banned from the castle! I only came here to make sure things were in order!" Adair screamed.

"Silence, fool! His majesty has ordered that any and all intruders be apprehended! There are no exceptions to this decree!" a guard shouted.

"It would seem that despite being explicitly warned not to show up unless you were on duty, you still decided to break my orders and come here. I suppose you have an excuse for this."

Hearing his cold and smooth voice, the guards who were not holding Adair captive saluted their king who walked into view with a smirk on his face.

"Greetings, your highness," one guard interjected. "We caught Adair sneaking through the barrier of magic that you cast over the castle. He claimed to have been concerned about security in the castle, but he was not supposed to be on duty today."

"Your majesty! I only came out of concern! Please, tell them to release me now!"

The Dark Fae king laughed. "How humorous. Do you really think that you can tell me what to do Adair?"

Before Adair could respond, the Dark Fae king cast a spell. Blue sparks crackled within his fingertips; the familiar scent of rhododendrons filled the air. Scenes from the past displayed themselves in the air.

One scene displayed Adair sneaking into the dungeons and freeing Heliodor; the other showed him speaking directly with Nessa. One of the most shocking scenes was that after Adair had freed Heliodor, he immediately created a shadow key for the Light Fae to be able to use to get inside the castle.

"You see, Adair, I know everything that goes on in my castle, including the little rendezvous you've been having with Nessa. The sad fact of this matter is that even if you had not shown up in my castle today, I would still have my guards arrest you and throw you in the dungeons!" Oren declared, knowing the main reason why Willow had even been captured by Heliodor in the first place was due to Adair's traitorous actions. It would only make sense to finally let the idiot know that he had been found out.

"Your services are no longer required, Adair. I know of everything that you have done, including the facilitation of Willow's kidnapping. After all, I know you were the one who set Heliodor free and allowed him back inside the castle."

Adair thought that Oren could still be convinced of his innocence, so he tried to plea with the Dark Fae king. "I don't know what you mean, your majesty. I did not allow anyone to kidnap the young lady, much less allow anyone into your castle. The

Light Fae escaped on his own."

The Dark Fae king chuckled darkly; the features of his face twisted into a wicked smile, sending a chilling message to Adair, who now looked very fearful of him. "You think that I, the high king and ruler of the Dark Fae Court, would ever let you go? You are very much mistaken. For you see, this time you're my prisoner. And this time, you won't be so lucky as to escape your fate. I know every single thing that you did, Adair, from sending Nessa information to letting Heliodor kidnap Willow." Oren motioned for his guards to bring the disgraced Fae in front of him.

The guards shoved Adair toward the ground, forcing him onto his knees. At this point, the Dark Fae knew that he would not be able to convince Oren that he had no connection to Nessa, but he decided to feign his innocence in hopes that the Dark Fae king would be lenient toward him.

Whilst most of the guards were distracted by the reappearance of Adair, no one noticed a shadowy figure making its way into the castle where the rest of Oren's guards stood.

Stopping in front of the guard's hall, the figure walked in. Seeing a lone guard with dark hair and green eyes, the figure pulled out a gold blowpipe and inserted a dart, aiming directly at his neck. A moment after the poisoned dart pierced the guard's neck, he lost consciousness and fell to the floor. The shadowy figure forced his mouth open, pulled out a vial filled with a purple liquid, and tipped its contents into the guard's mouth, forcing him so swallow it. A few minutes later the guard jolted awake. Deeming the task to be successful, the figure melted into the shadows once more, leaving no trace behind.

The guard's mind was completely blank; he stood up and looked around in bewilderment.

Ah, so your name is Alder. You shall be under my control. Your job is to keep an eye on Willow and carry out a small task for me, a cold voice spoke inside his mind, one that the guard immediately recognized as belonging to the Dwarf queen.

Simply nodding to no one in particular, the Dark Fae guard stood up and walked out of the room, silently trailing the halls, waiting for the chance to follow Willow.

"No! Your majesty! Please! I'm innocent! Perhaps Willow has put a spell on you and clouded your judgement!" Adair tried to reason.

Oren narrowed his eyes at the sniveling creature in front of him and suddenly reached out, grabbing him by his neck and lifting him off the ground. Immediately, Adair started gasping for air as he felt the oxygen leaving his body.

"Listen carefully, as I doubt you have the brain cells to comprehend the words leaving my mouth. Don't ever blame Willow for the wickedness that is in your heart. You made a personal choice to betray my kingdom! How dare you stand before me and beg me to spare you! I should kill you right now, but that would be too merciful for the likes of you!"

By now, Adair was utterly suffocated and thus had become unconscious while Oren was talking.

He unceremoniously dumped Adair's barely living body to the ground and gestured to his guards. "Take this filth away and lock him up in the dungeons. I will be there shortly to take care of things."

"Yes, your highness. Right away." The guards hauled the unconscious Dark Fae toward the dungeons, respectfully nodding to Oren as they left.

"The rest of you, gather more guards and continue rotations. I don't want to see a single creature or individual enter my castle without my explicit permission or else they will find themselves meeting the exact same fate as Adair! Do I make myself perfectly clear?" Oren met the gazes of every single guard that was standing in the vicinity, daring someone to speak out against him.

"We understand, your majesty!" they all chorused in unison.

After hearing that, the Dark Fae king turned on his heels and left the courtyard, making his way back inside the castle and toward the rooms of his family and friend. As soon as he stepped into the view of the hall where the room stood, he was met by a slightly worried Nerida, who came up to him, her red and black nightgown swishing about her and her hair down.

"Oren, darling, what happened? I heard shouting coming from the courtyard," she said.

"It was an intruder, dearest. Adair to be specific. He thought he was clever, trying to worm his way back into my castle. No doubt he came to kidnap Willow once more. I taught him a lesson and he is currently in the dungeons."

Nerida's anger flared a little, but she immediately forced herself to remain calm. "I see. Is Willow alright? I know he wasn't able to make his way inside, but the thought of Willow in danger boils my blood. Not to mention that he can produce shadow keys, being in the dungeons means nothing to him."

Oren gently grasped Nerida's hand, placing a kiss on the back. "There is no need to worry, I took care of it. The castle is under heavy enchantments, and the dungeons no longer have physical locks. I've replaced them all with magical seals, all of which can only be opened by me."

Her cheeks coloring slightly, she continued. "Willow is safe then?"

"Yes, my dear butterfly. She's inside her room."

"Mom, Dad, is everything okay? I heard a lot of screaming voices," a small voice said behind them. Nerida and Oren turned to see Wisp standing in the doorway of their room, her pale pink nightgown slightly ruffled and her dark hair messy. She sleepily rubbed her mismatched eyes as she looked at her parents.

"Don't worry about it, my little flower. Your father has taken care of everything." Nerida gestured her daughter to come closer, wrapping her arms around the little Dark Fae princess when she did so.

"When can I see Willow, Dad? You promised me that after you rescued her, I could see her."

Oren chuckled at his daughter's enthusiasm; after all, the young princess hadn't been able to spend time with Willow due to unforeseen circumstances.

"Don't worry, my little flower petal, you'll see her when we eat breakfast," Oren reassured her.

"Alright then. I'll get ready!" she squealed. As quickly as she had come, Wisp ran back to her room, presumably get ready for the day.

"Let me get dressed too, dear. You can go and take Willow to the dining hall," said Nerida. Pressing one last kiss to Nerida's hand and laughing as her cheeks heated up in a fierce blush, the Dark Fae king walked toward Willow's room.

He knocked on the door and a worried Willow hesitantly opened the door a crack before throwing it open upon seeing that it was the Dark Fae king.

"Is everything alright, Oren? Who was screaming?" Willow was concerned for Oren's well-being, and the screams she heard did nothing to assuage her fears.

"Worry not my dear. It was just an intruder. He'll soon find himself a permanent guest in my new dungeon," Oren explained.

A confused look passed by on her face before she realized exactly who the Dark Fae king was talking about. "You finally caught Adair, right?" she asked.

Oren nodded. "I did indeed, my dear. He thought he could make his way into my castle without notice. I've no doubt that he came here to kidnap you under orders from Nessa."

Willow inwardly sighed; it was starting to become apparent that the Dwarf queen had an unhealthy obsession with her many attempts to destroy Oren. "I don't understand what's so special about me. You said that my power is unlike a normal Faeling's, and even Nessa said I was incredibly powerful. But I've never used my powers on my own volition, well, except when I was trying to escape from Nessa's kingdom."

Oren could understand the young woman's frustrations, she'd been thrust into a realm that was dealing with its own fair share of problems, and the icing on the metaphorical cake was that she had powers that somehow tied her into the middle of the chaos.

"I can't say for certain why your powers are this way, Willow. But perhaps we can find something in the library and archives. The archives may have something about your parents that could explain why your powers seem to be stronger than a normal Faeling's," he said.

Before she could respond, the Dark Fae princess practically skipped into view, wearing a pale pink dress adorned with silver dragonflies and matching slippers. Her pendant rested around her neck and her dark hair was held up by a shiny pink ribbon.

"Are you coming now, Dad? Or do you still have to talk to Willow?" she asked with a serious face.

Laughing, Oren picked up his daughter and pressed a quick kiss to her cheek. "Whatever am I going to do with you, precious petal? Why don't you go and find your mother? Willow and I will be down shortly."

Staring at her father for a moment, she nodded her head. "Alright, Dad. I'll be waiting for you."

She turned and walked down the hall until she was no longer in Oren's sight.

"Well then, my dear. I'll let you freshen up and then you can come down the hall for breakfast. If you cannot find your way, let my guards know. They will gladly bring you to the dining hall," he shared with a smile.

"Thank you, Oren. I'll be down soon."

Oren turned and left, leaving Willow standing in the doorway. She watched his form disappear down the hallway before shutting the door to her room and making her way toward the bathroom. Once inside, she took a quick bath, rinsing her dark hair with a shampoo that smelled like jasmine and using a soap that smelled like roses. After stepping out of the bathroom, she deftly brushed her hair and tied it back with a silver ribbon. She pulled on a matching silver tunic that was embroidered with blue flowers and matching blue pants. After glancing at the boots in the closet, she decided to pull on a pair of gray ones that had a charm of a rose on the side.

Willow made her way down the halls. Walking down a set of stairs, she finally found her way into the dining hall where Oren, Nerida, and Wisp were sitting.

"Willow! I'm so glad I get to finally meet you properly!" the young princess said. She was so excited that she threw her arms around Willow in an unexpected hug.

Willow chuckled and hugged the little princess. "I'm glad to properly meet you too, Wisp."

The princess tugged Willow's hand and gestured for her to sit in the seat next to her. "My dad has told me a lot about you. He says you're very brave and smart. I think so, too. Who else would be smart enough to trick that old toad Nessa?"

"Wisp, honey, I understand that you don't like Nessa but don't say things like that," Nerida corrected.

Wisp looked sheepish for a moment. "Sorry, Mom. I'm just angry that she hurt Willow."

"That's sweet of you, and after breakfast, you can take her out to the gardens." Nerida smiled as she handed everyone each a plate that had eggs and toast. Then she poured cups of butterfly pea flower tea, which was colored a sapphire blue.

As they ate, Wisp and Willow talked about numerous things, including their favorite colors, foods, flowers, and books. After they had finished eating, Wisp tugged Willow's hand and tried to lead her to the gardens, much to Nerida and Oren's amusement.

"Wisp, sweetie, be careful when you go out with Willow. I want you to come straight back inside after you're done," Nerida directed.

The princess nodded. She knew that because of the many incidents that had been happening, her mother was worried about her safety. "Alright, Mom. I promise I'll come straight back."

In the gardens, Wisp impressed Willow with her knowledge of flowers and plants, and Wisp even pointed out the ones that could be used in healing and making teas. A short while passed and Oren found the two of them giggling with each other as they pointed to the clouds in the sky.

"I see you're having fun, precious petal. However, I do have to borrow Willow for a little bit. Why don't you go inside for now?" he proposed. Wisp sighed but understood.

"I'll go inside then. See you later, Willow." With the flap of her little wings, the princess made her way back inside the castle.

Oren offered his arm to Willow. "Shall we go to the library and archives, my dear?"

Taking his offered arm, the two of them made their way inside the library, hoping to find the answers to the questions that remained largely unanswered.

Where had Willow's powers come from if she had lived in the human realm her whole life? And was there something about herself that even she didn't know?

CHAPTER 16

Willow and Oren made their way past the ornate halls of his castle, thoughtfully silent as they came to a set of ash-colored doors embellished with silver and purple dragonflies. Pulling open the doors, which had silver handles shaped like dragonfly wings, Oren revealed a large room with many books and archived records, some of which seemed to appear by the minute.

Large windows lined the room, some bringing in sunlight, some depicting the many courts within the realm. Much to Willow's surprise, the figures in the stained glass windows moved, and when they saw Oren walk into the room, they all stopped what they were doing and respectfully nodded their heads toward the Dark Fae king.

Willow looked around in awe. Oren's library and archive was much grander and more magnificent than the ones she had seen back in the human realm. But then again, her library wasn't in a magical realm. Aside from the shelves of books and records, there were many ornate silver desks stacked with stationary and writing utensils, and the chairs were a rich shade of purple.

"This room is amazing!" Willow exclaimed, taking a slow circle to take in the room around her.

The Dark Fae king chuckled at her enthusiasm. "I'm glad you like it, my dear. This is a special room. Any time a book is written anywhere in any place, it appears here. The same thing goes for any records about families, historical events, and so forth."

Willow turned to look at Oren. "How do the archives work?" she inquired.

Without a word, Oren walked over to a specific section that looked a bit more intricate than some of the other ones and pulled out a silver-colored paper with a family tree that—much to Willow's surprise and confusion—was blank. Noticing her confused gaze, the Dark Fae king moved to explain.

"You asked how the archives worked, my dear. I will show you, as well as explain afterward." Hovering a finger over the paper, Oren took out his blade and pricked the tip. A small droplet of his ink-black blood fell onto the parchment. Suddenly, many names and pictures appeared, including Oren's own. Most interesting of all was that the type of creature also appeared next to the names. For Oren, it showed that he was a Dark Fae. A couple of the names were faded, prompting Willow's curiosity. "Why are a few of the names on the tree faded?"

"The faded names represent those who are no longer in the realm of the living. Any living member from the family can reveal their entire history just by a single droplet of blood. There really is no other way to reveal an individual's parentage, as the blood running in the family's veins is the only way to unlock the secrets of the family tree," the Dark Fae king answered.

Willow was in awe, it wasn't like the history archives back home where everything had to be recorded by the living members of the family to ensure that no one was forgotten, although this was a magical realm, so it made sense that things would be this way.

"Is my family tree here, too?" Willow was curious to know which of her parents was the Fae.

Oren nodded and walked over to another shelf, pulling out another silver piece of parchment. He motioned for Willow to come over, although the Dark Fae king was feeling a sort of hesitation. He didn't want to put Willow through any unnecessary pain, and the thought of drawing her blood, though a small amount it was, made him uneasy.

Seeing a fountain pen in the collection of writing utensils that was on the desk, Willow grabbed it and pricked the tip of her finger, much to Oren's shock. A ruby-red drop of blood fell onto the parchment, and just like the Dark Fae king's family tree, names, pictures, and types of creatures appeared on the parchment as well.

Before she could say anything, Oren grabbed her hand, and with a spark of sapphire, healed the finger that she had just pricked. "You shouldn't have done that so suddenly. At least give me a fair warning next time, my dear," he said.

Willow rolled her eyes. "I'm not made of glass, you know. There's no need for you to worry so much." Willow glanced down at the parchment. Her eyes widened in shock, and she began to feel dizzy.

The names of her parents read: Fiore and Elowen. *Dark Fae*

was written next to both of their names. Although, both of her parent's names were faded.

Seeing Willow go quiet all of sudden, the Dark Fae king looked down at the parchment to see Willow's parentage. Oren's face went white. He glanced over to Willow, who had begun to panic.

"My parents . . . they can't be my parents. My mother's name is Rowan, and my father's name is Florian. And they're both alive. I have siblings, I'm not an only child. How is this possible? I can't be a Dark Fae!" Willow sputtered.

Seeing her distressed, the Dark Fae king guided the young woman to a chair, made her sit down, and crouched in front of her, gently grabbing her hands once more. After a few moments, Willow's breath slowed, and her eyes lifted to meet Oren's.

"Breathe, Willow. We will figure this out, I promise you. But you need to calm down before you make yourself sick. After all, you've barely recovered."

Taking a deep breath, Willow calmed herself further, although her confusion and concern didn't waver.

"The archives hold more than just family trees. They also hold information that has happened in the history of this realm and even your hometown if individuals from this realm are involved. There has to be something written about your parents." The Dark Fae king stood up and strode over to the shelves and cast a spell, purple sparks leaving his fingertips, the scent of lilacs filling the air.

The purple sparks hovered over every shelf until they came to a stop and engulfed a specific section of records. The purple sparks then brought the records over to where Willow sat.

Oren's eyes flickered toward a familiar-looking seal sitting on top of the records, but he shook off his surprise before Willow noticed.

"I can use a spell that will bring these records to life if you'd like, my dear. It would be much faster than trying to read them all," Oren suggested, a tinge or worry still in his eyes.

Willow nodded with apprehension. She steadied herself for what she was about to learn about her life. "That's fine with me. Either way, I want to know what happened to them."

With a wave of his hands, a pleasant scent of jasmine flowers filled the air. The Dark Fae king was astonished that the seal allowed him to view the records locked inside, thinking that perhaps Willow had to be the one to open it. Nevertheless, both Willow and Oren were transported back into the past, one that Willow had no idea existed.

CHAPTER 17

Flowers bloomed everywhere—on the hills, the trees, and even on the grass, which was lush and green; this was a herald to spring. Two figures walked along the blossoming paths, each holding the hand of what appeared to be a little girl.

One of the figures was dressed in a powder blue tunic with silver pants, the silver embroidery reminiscent of leaves. Around his hip was a silver scabbard that held a sword with a deep blue hilt, engraved with roses in a midnight color. His wings were the color of the ocean on a sunny day, resembling that of a butterfly's. His eyes were the color of the night sky, as was his hair, which reached down to his shoulders, hanging loosely. He also wore black riding boots adorned with chains that rattled each time he walked, much to the delight of the little girl gripping his hand.

The other figure was dressed in a white gown, the black embroidery reminiscent of leafy vines, and she wore slippers that matched. Over her shoulder hung a black satchel, golden with designs of stars and constellations. Her eyes were dark brown, her hair the same, reaching down past her shoulders in a long braid adorned with tiny jasmine flowers. Much like the figure in blue, she also had wings reminiscent of a butterfly, except they were white in color.

The little girl holding each of their hands wore a pink tunic embroidered with tiny silver butterflies and black pants. Her slippers, which were the same color as her tunic, were also adorned with silver butterflies. She looked like a smaller version of the figure in the white gown, with the exception of her hair, which was pulled back in a small ponytail that had a jasmine flower tucked into the top, and her wings, which were pink and black with traces of white spots that sparkled like opals in the sun. Seeing a black-and-blue butterfly, she released the two hands that she was holding and chased after it. When she was out of earshot, the figure in the white gown turned to the one in the powder blue tunic with a worried look.

"Fiore, I don't think we're safe staying in the Dark Fae kingdom any longer," she whispered.

Fiore turned toward her, his gaze a bit worried, yet still filled with love and adoration.

"I know, Elowen. I can sense the restlessness from King Faven's spies. The Light Fae really would do anything to get me to reveal the secrets of his majesty's castle. Faven even offered to shield our family from his majesty's wrath if I told him of the many twists and turns inside the castle. I would never betray my king to that swamp toad."

Elowen sighed, watching the little girl chasing the butterfly. "Why did you have to be the royal architect? All this could have been avoided if you didn't have the knowledge of the inner workings of his castle," Elowen said, a look of distress on her face.

Fiore smiled, taking Elowen's hands into his own, and gently wiped away the tears that started forming in the corners of her eyes.

"I was the royal architect long before I met you, my dearest jasmine flower," he replied. "It's something I quite enjoy. As for designing the castle, Oren and I go way back; ever since we were young Fae, he and I have been the best of friends. So, when he asked if I could redesign his castle and build something better, I took the challenge."

Elowen wiped her eyes, once more glancing toward her daughter who had grown tired from chasing the butterfly and had sat down on a smooth grey rock formation in the grass. "If he's your oldest and closet friend, why does he not offer us protection against the Light Fae king? Surely, he must know of the incredible amount of danger our family is in," she said.

Fiore sighed.

"If Oren was aware of the danger we were in, then he most certainly would offer his protection. Sadly, because the Light Fae and Dwarves have constantly been threatening to go to war with the Dark Fae Court, he does not know of this. Besides, this is just a small drop of water compared to the issues he has to deal with. However, I did leave my notes with him. At least in that, the Light Fae won't go looking for something I don't have possession of."

Elowen sighed tiredly. "Between the constant threats of war and the feeling of being watched at every turn, I'm exhausted,

Fiore. And the fact that Oren has your notes changes nothing. They will still come after us."

"I know you're exhausted, but Oren can't protect us as well as the kingdom. We must think of a way to keep our family safe. As for the notes, I gave them to him so that at least he would be safe," Fiore responded.

"I suppose it's better than having them with us. However, something must be done so that we can ensure Willow's safety first. Who knows what will happen to us later on?" she said.

Fiore thought for a moment. While he couldn't fathom the idea of not being able to protect his family, Elowen was correct. They needed some sort of plan to ensure that at least Willow would be safe. Looking around, Fiore cast a spell that sparkled with a violet light and left the scent of lavender in the air.

"No one will be able to hear us now. We can speak freely without fear of Faven's spies listening in on the conversation." Fiore sat down by the same rock formation that his daughter was sitting on, though he was a bit further away so that Willow wouldn't hear the conversation between them. Patting the patch of grass next to him, he gestured for Elowen to come and sit by him. Elowen walked over and sat down, looking around the clearing cautiously.

"Are you certain that no one can hear us?" she asked.

"Rest assured, my dearest. I learned the spell from Oren himself," he replied.

Elowen glanced around the area once more, hoping that at least they could have a moment of peace, if only to discuss how they would make sure Willow was taken care of.

"I think we should send Willow to the human realm. She's less likely to be found since there is no record of any magic being used in that place," Elowen suggested.

Fiore was a bit hesitant to send his only child to a strange place. "Does it have to be in the human realm? And how is a child as small as Willow supposed to take care of herself there?" he replied.

Elowen turned to the satchel that she had been carrying and pulled out a small black book with gold lettering. "Do you remember that I told you my family comes from a long line of healers? That we discovered that if you incorporated certain flowers or plants within a spell, almost any injury could instantly be healed? Well, my mother specialized in healing an individual's memories; in fact, she is the inventor of the many spells that are widely used now. But did you know that if you were to change a certain plant for one that looked similar, it would create the opposite effect?"

Fiore looked at Elowen, a look of both curiosity and shock evident on his face.

"Are you suggesting that we alter Willow's memories after we leave her in the human realm? Is that not dangerous? Is the spell reversible?" he inquired.

Elowen thumbed through the book that she had been holding, and the look of relief that passed on her face reassured Fiore. "It can most certainly be reversed. The cure for *The Spell of the Forgotten* is on the opposite page."

"Mom, Dad, look! The butterfly is sitting on my head!" A small voice interrupted their conversation, both of them glancing in their daughter's direction.

She giggled at the butterfly, which had taken to perching itself on her head. Elowen and Fiore laughed despite everything; the conversation was momentarily forgotten as they walked over to where Willow was sitting. The butterfly on her head flew off as soon as her parents approached, much to the young girl's disappointment.

"Aww! It flew away!" she said. She moved to chase after the creature once more, but her mother stopped her.

"Your father and I need to talk to you about something, Willow," Elowen said softly.

Fiore and Elowen shared a look and nodded at each other. "Your mother and I want you to know that we love you very much," Fiore began.

"Something's wrong, isn't it?" Willow was too smart for her own good. Even at her age she noted the tension and constant danger they were in, though she did not know the extent.

"You guessed right, my little petal. It's just that we don't have much time before things become very dangerous. Your father and I can't protect you here for much longer," Elowen shared.

"We were thinking of taking you to the human realm for now," Fiore added.

Willow looked at her mother, her body trembling and her eyes shiny and filled with unshed tears. Both her parents pulled the young girl into a hug, her mother stroking her hair, while her father murmured words of comfort. "I can promise that you'll be safe in the human realm, Willow." Willow stared at her father with sadness evident in her eyes.

"You and Mom and won't be coming with me, though. How

can you say that I'll be safe if you won't be there?" she asked. She began sobbing silently in her parents' arms.

Elowen sighed. Willow understood the circumstances they were presenting to her, which only made things harder. Elowen and Fiore needed to get her to the human realm as soon as possible and far away from the Dark Fae Court for her own safety. Flipping to the page with the spell they intended to use, Elowen scanned it to see what they'd need.

"*The Spell of the Forgotten* requires pinxter azalea. That flower is commonly found in the human realm. The cure to this spell is sweet azalea, which I have in the greenhouse." Fiore nodded. "We'll head back home and prepare to collect the flower we need from the human realm. There isn't any danger to this spell is there?"

Elowen shook her head. "I wouldn't use this spell if I wasn't absolutely sure."

Fiore let out a small sigh, something that he rarely did unless he was really worried. "I fear tampering with Willow's memories will cause her to forget more than just us. Are you also planning on taking away her memories of magic? The notes in the margin of the page say that if you cause a Fae to forget that they belong to this realm, then they lose their wings and connection to the life force of their magical abilities. I haven't even started to teach Willow about her power yet," Fiore reflected, as the three of them walked back to the hidden glade of the forest where their home was.

"We don't have much of a choice. The Light Fae will stop at nothing to eliminate us because they see your refusal to give them information on Oren as a personal offense, especially when being offered power and wealth by their king. It's best if Willow doesn't remember any of this, as it would break her heart to know that she lost her parents for a senseless reason."

Looking at their daughter who happened to be tightly clinging to both of her parents, Fiore contemplated what his wife said. "What of placing her in the human's realm? We can't just let her wander around aimlessly; she's too young to be left alone," Fiore said.

While Willow and Oren were under the spell, watching the memories of her mother and father, Alder, one of Oren's guards, stood in the shadows, silently watching them. With a wave of his hand, the windows shattered.

CRASH!

The sound of shattered glass broke the reverie of the spell Oren had cast, interrupting the memory that Willow had been watching. Immediately, upon hearing the crash, the Dark Fae king pulled Willow behind him and drew a silver sword from the nearby wall. Oren assumed that Alder must have been thrown in through the window, his battered form bleeding onto the floor from the many cuts that littered his body. His dark hair spilled out in all directions, and his green eyes looked weakly toward Oren as he tried to relay a message.

"Your majesty . . . the Light Fae . . . attack . . . war . . ."

Acting quickly, Oren cast a spell, and silver sparks appeared on the tips of his fingers as he aimed them at the fallen Dark Fae. The wounds on the body of the guard healed, and he rose quickly, almost as if he had never been hurt in the first place.

"Alder, tell me what exactly happened," Oren demanded.

"Your highness! The Light Fae have started gathering an army along with their allies. They plan to attack us and our allies in a few months. I was unfortunate enough to be caught by them and then sent back as an example of what happens to those that oppose Nessa and Heliodor," Alder explained.

The sword in Oren's hand broke as he shook with rage. "If it's a war that they want, then I suppose we'll have to indulge them, won't we?" He smirked with each word that he spoke. "Alder, send a message out to our allies and tell them we are to have an emergency meeting. It is mandatory."

The guard nodded his head, turning toward the exit of the library and archives. While he walked out, an evil smirk spread on his face as soon as he turned away from the king.

With a wave of his hand, Oren repaired the broken window. Softening his gaze, he turned to Willow and saw that the young woman had tears forming in the corners of her eyes. Gently wiping them away, he sat her down on the chair once more.

Oren was also in shock—the young woman in front of him was the daughter of his closest friend.

"I had no idea you were Fiore's daughter. Had I known who you were and where you had been, I would have tried much sooner to help you understand your powers and history," the Dark Fae king explained.

"I believe you, Oren. He said it himself in the memory, he didn't want to burden you when you already had issues with the Light Court," Willow said.

Oren sighed wistfully. Both Fiore and his daughter were alike in so many ways, how could he have missed that?

"Why didn't you look at the archives before?" Willow asked with a perplexed look on her face.

Luckily for himself, the Dark Fae king was prepared for that question.

"When I received word that your father was no longer in the realm of the living, I was devastated. Unfortunately, the archived records would only allow a living member of his family to access it. The spell I used to find your family records is how I was able to pick the correct one. I will admit, I was surprised when I saw Fiore's records appear after I had cast the spell."

Oren was fearful that Willow wouldn't want to associate with him if she thought that he was purposefully withholding information from her.

Willow sighed sadly. She had finally found out the truth, and if it wasn't for Oren, she might not have ever known. "I trust you, Oren. You were close friends with my parents. This doesn't change anything between us, we are and always will be friends."

A look of relief was evident on the Dark Fae king's face at those words. "I thank you for your kind words, my dear. I know you would most likely prefer to view the rest of the records, but I have to make sure the message gets sent out for the meeting tomorrow."

Willow stood up, smiling. "Let's take care of Nessa and

Heliodor first, then we can come back. It's not like we won't be able to access the records once we're done anyways."

Standing up from where he had been seated, the Dark Fae king and the newly discovered Dark Fae walked out of the room to prepare for the meeting—a meeting that would show how well the Dark Alliance would react to this news and whether they would be prepared to defend their courts alongside Oren.

CHAPTER 18

Voices shouted left and right, some celebratory and some accusatory. The dimly lit room did nothing to reveal which voice belonged to whom. The sound of weapons and armor clinking in the room added more to the already growing chaos and restlessness of the inhabitants inside.

"Where's Queen Nessa? I grow tired of waiting for her to show up each time she calls us here! And why is it always so dark in this hall?" King Nash complained.

"Shut up, Nash! I'm sick of hearing you complain! You live underground anyways; it's always dark!" Prince Sol retorted.

"How many times must I explain to you, ignorant little Sun Elf, we Goblins live in a fortress that is in no way, shape, or form located below the ground! It would do you well to update those idiotic fairy tales of yours!" he snapped back.

"That's enough! Shut up and sit down! No one wants to hear your petty arguments!" Heliodor interrupted.

After what seemed like an eternity, Nessa finally walked into the room, a golden sword with peridots on the hilt and engravings of nightshade on the blade dangling from her hip. She wore a gold dress with elaborate embroidery reminiscent of the same flowers on her sword. Her hair hung loosely on her shoulders, and her usual crown perched on her head, the rings on her fingers sparkling in the dim light. The voices hushed somewhat as the Dwarf queen sat down on an elaborate chair of gold and green.

"I've gathered you all here today to tell you that we've practically won the war with Oren and his allies. All we must do is stage our attack, and then we claim the courts who tried to go against us for ourselves."

King Nash looked doubtful. After the first few failures of the Light Alliance, he wasn't so sure they would win against the high king.

"Are you quite certain of this, Queen Nessa? After failing to kill Oren and failing to get the girl under control, what makes you think that we can win against him? He always seems to be ten steps ahead of us whenever we make plans to destroy him," he said.

Queen Nessa narrowed her eyes at the Goblin king before bursting out in malicious laughter. "Don't underestimate me, King Nash. Oren is strong and seemingly invincible, but I can assure you he has a weakness. That weakness happens to be the Dark Fae, Willow."

Nash interrupted. "What do you mean Dark Fae? I thought she wasn't a full-fledged Fae . . ." Nash trailed off in confusion.

Nessa chuckled darkly; it was good to have more than one spy in place. "Do you remember how we sent someone to Oren's castle while Adair made an appearance? One of Oren's guards drank a special tea with deadly nightshade, a spell that will keep him under my control for a few weeks. He has been spying on Oren and his little friend for quite some time, and the fool suspects nothing. As for how I figured out the girl is a full-fledged Dark Fae, I had placed a spell on Alder so that I would be able to view what he sees. Apparently before Heliodor killed King Faven, the old fool had been planning to kill Oren's architect and the architect's family. Alder saw the same things that the Dark Fae saw in the memory archives, and she now knows that she isn't a Faeling."

Prince Sol scoffed at the mere mention of Willow. "You don't even have her in your grasp, and yet somehow, she is still a part of your plans in the grand scheme of things. We're just wasting our time with a useless individual!"

A cold voice spoke out, chilling the very air, ceasing all sounds, as the chatter died down. "You're forgetting one very important thing, Prince Sol. Since the young woman is a full Fae and not half, her magic is considered very powerful. Since she didn't spend time in this realm as a child, her powers only grew in strength with no real way to be released. This is a buildup of pressure . . . for those who need simpler terminology. As such, her magic comes out in bursts of energy when it senses she is in danger." Lord Obsidian stepped into view, his dark green tunic with embroidery of white candytufts glinting in the dim light.

"This is complete and utter nonsense. If she was a Faeling, she would be powerful, and now that she's a Dark Fae she's still the same! Do we even need her at this point? And who in their right minds would be subjected to believe such nonsensical information?" said Prince Sol, exasperated.

Lord Obsidian smirked. These creatures still hadn't given him a proper reason for wanting to go to war with Oren, and it was amusing to watch them squirm and argue with one another each time he relayed new information.

"Prince Sol, I suggest you read the books in your library, that is, if you even have one. You don't necessarily need the individual; there is a way to drain the power. But it comes at a cost, the power is less effective when not being wielded by its owner. That is why it's better to have the individual on your side," explained Obsidian.

"If it's so nonsensical, why don't you do your own research, Prince Sol?" a voice chimed in, belonging to none other than the Shapeshifter queen, Calista.

"That's enough! I grow tired of hearing your petty squabbles. Listen to me carefully, all of you!

"With Alder under my control, I plan on having him use the same spell that I used, except Oren's little friend will ingest the plant part. This is going to ensure that she stays under my control. Are there any objections?" Nessa asked. She glanced around the room, its inhabitants all silent, no one daring to disagree with the Dwarf queen.

"Very well. This meeting is adjourned, and I would suggest that all of you be ready in the next few days or so to reconvene here once more when I finally have the girl under my control."

With those words spoken, Nessa got up from her seat and left the hall, not waiting to see if any of the leaders from the alliance left. Prince Sol stood up, the legs of his chair scraping against the floor, his whole body shaking with rage at Lord Obsidian's mockery of his intelligence. For once, he wordlessly strode out of the room and presumably went back to his court, no doubt to brush off the dust on the books in his library. The other leaders followed suit, with only Heliodor remaining in the room.

Casting a glance at the room, he waved his hand as orange sparks flew from his fingertips and cleared the mess left behind by everyone. Perhaps this would earn him more favor, as Nessa didn't like seeing her room being left in disarray. He really hoped that Nessa would be able to pull her plan off, otherwise they would lose allies, and everyone would start fighting amongst themselves in an effort to become the high ruler.

Alder walked the halls of Oren's castle, carrying a cup of lavender-colored tea, a strong floral aroma coming from the steam that left the cup. His eyes held a strange violet glint to them as he walked down the hallways, as if he was possessed by something.

He looked around for Willow. The tea in his hands was meant to deliver a blow to the Dark Fae king . . . if he could get Willow to drink it. Nessa had ordered Alder to make sure she would drink it, even if it had to be done by force. Frustrated that he couldn't seem to find her, he turned the corner of the hallway, and ran right into the very person he had been seeking.

She was chatting with Lady Anthea, and the both of them

showed no signs of stopping the conversation. There would be no way for him to slip the tainted tea to the young woman without raising suspicions. Gritting his teeth in frustration and gripping the teacup tightly, he turned and stalked off in the direction of Willow's room. He opened the door a crack before peering inside. Seeing that the room was empty for the moment, he placed the cup on the table. Grabbing a piece of silver paper and a pen, he wrote a note, folded the paper, and placed it next to the cup. After doing so, he made sure that no one was out in the hallway, then he swiftly left the room and resumed his duties without any suspicion. Night soon fell, and Willow came back to her room, spotting the cup of tea alongside the note on the table. Piqued with curiosity, she picked up the note and unfolded it, eyes scanning over the words.

Dearest Willow,

I brought you some lavender tea whilst you were away. It should help provide for an excellent night's sleep. When we have the time, I promise you that I will answer all questions you have about your father.

Sincerely,

Oren

She folded the note closed once more, contemplating the words written inside. Hadn't he already promised her that they would watch the rest of the records? Up until he had seen the family tree, the Dark Fae king didn't know she was Fiore's daughter. Thinking that maybe he just said those words to soothe any hurt in her heart, the young woman hesitantly picked up the teacup, inhaling the floral scent of lavender. Unbeknownst to her, Alder had come back and was watching her through the crack of the slightly open door.

Raising the cup to her lips, she took a sip of the tea, the taste of something floral with hints of mint and rosemary washing over her tongue. Deciding that she liked the flavor, the young woman downed the entire cup, falling asleep afterward.

Alder, upon seeing this, quickly reported back to Nessa. Now all that Nessa had to do was wait until morning and Willow would be under her control until either the Dwarf queen released her from the spell, or the young woman broke free on her own. Both options were quite unlikely, of this Nessa was certain.

As night was falling, all the inhabitants of the castle were getting ready to sleep, not including the guards who were scheduled to patrol at night. As Oren was preparing for bed, he couldn't help but think that something was feeling quite off, almost as if there was a storm about to hit. Nerida had long fallen asleep, no doubt she had been exhausted from the events happening in the realm, so Oren couldn't discuss his musings until morning. Sighing quietly, he quickly dressed himself for bed and slid soundlessly under the blankets, letting a restless sleep claim him for the night.

CHAPTER 19

The day started off with a strange feeling in the air. The sun hid itself, and dark clouds loomed in the skies instead. Oren woke up as usual, but the feeling that something was off that he had before bed the night before persisted. Try as he might, the Dark Fae king couldn't quite pinpoint the reason for his unease. Getting out of bed, he pulled on a plum-colored tunic with intricate embroidery reminiscent of silver butterflies, black pants, and purple boots that had the same silvery butterfly pattern. Gently shaking Nerida awake, he ran a brush through his ink-black locks.

Nerida yawned and got up, dressing herself in clothing that was in similar colors to the ones that the Dark Fae king was wearing, the exception being that her hair was tied in a long braid with a purple-and-silver ribbon and that she was wearing a dress and slippers with designs of silvery butterflies.

"Something doesn't quite feel right. I can see the look in your eyes, Oren," Nerida said.

Oren glanced at her, their eyes meeting.

"Indeed. We need to be prepared for anything that happens," he responded.

"I'll go and dress Wisp, then I'll meet you downstairs, Oren darling," she said, placing a kiss on his cheek before she left the room.

While they had a feeling that something was wrong, they were both unaware of the turmoil that the day would bring.

As the Dark Fae king walked the halls toward the dining area, he noticed the castle was eerily silent—not a single guard was to be found where they usually were.

When he arrived at the dining hall, he saw Willow's figure sitting in one of the chairs with a small leatherbound book in her hands. However, Willow looked entirely different.

She wore a black tunic embroidered with red dahlias and crimson-colored pants to match. A leather jacket with gold chains rested on top of her shoulders. Her outfit was completed with black boots that had the same chains.

On her eye lids, there was a smokey grey and red eyeshadow, and her lips were stained black. Even her nails had been painted black. She wore red pearl earrings, accompanied by many other piercings, not unlike the ones Oren usually wore, except those were gold instead of silver.

Even her hair, which was usually done up in a simple pony-tail, hung loosely around her shoulders.

When she heard Oren's footsteps approaching, she promptly closed the book, and looked up, a smirk very much evident on her face.

"Ah, Oren. I was wondering when you'd finally show up." The voice that left those blackened lips sounded nothing like the sweet young woman that Oren knew. Instead, she sounded full of coldness and cruelty.

"Where did you get that book, Willow? And where are the guards?" Oren asked in confusion and concern.

Willow crossed her legs and chuckled darkly. "What's the matter, Oren? You don't like the new me? No usual 'my dear'? I bet you liked the other Willow, right? The one who sat sweetly and didn't question a single action of yours? Well, I have news for you, high king. There's a new Willow in this realm and that's me. Since you thought it was prudent to hide that you knew my father, I decided to team up with someone who wouldn't lie to me. This book is my father's journal, I think it's only fair that I get to keep it. And as for your silly little guards, I've put them to sleep, for now anyways. Can't have any witnesses to our little conversation now, can we?"

The silence was deafening as soon as the words left Willow's lips because Oren knew exactly who she had teamed with.

"You are joking, right? Are you perhaps ill?" the Dark Fae king asked, his eyes looking over at Willow in concern. He knew she would've been affected by the events that had occurred yesterday, but he didn't think that she would go so far as to pull something like this with him.

Willow burst out laughing. "Perhaps you're the one who's ill.

Can you simply not comprehend the fact that I can change sides, should I choose to do so?"

Oren's confusion and concern only increased with her answer. "You could have asked me for the book, Willow. There was no need for you to peruse through my study without my permission," Oren said.

Willow scoffed. "I don't need your permission, Oren. You're not in charge of me or where I go."

"I would think that you do need permission before going through the rooms in my castle. Had you simply asked me anything regarding your father, I would have brought you that journal," Oren answered calmly.

A dark laugh escaped from the young woman's mouth. She inspected her nails briefly before standing up, book in hand, a smirk forming on her face. "Why didn't you just mention my father's journal in the first place? Were you scared that since you'd abandoned his only daughter, she would leave after finding out the truth?"

Oren narrowed his eyes at the girl in front of him. This behavior had taken a sharp turn, and he had a slight feeling that she was not acting this way because of yesterday's events.

"Why don't you just tell me what the real problem is, Willow? Why go through all these theatrics?" he inquired.

Willow chuckled darkly. "You still don't get it, do you? The Willow you think you knew is gone! This is who I am now! The fact that you think this is some sort of joke really speaks volumes on your intelligence. It's like you can't believe I have the mind to join Nessa," she shared.

Oren responded calmly. "I choose to believe that you would not join forces with someone who had you kidnapped whilst under my care and then deliberately harmed you because of your refusal to join them in the first place."

Nessa scoffed inside of Willow's mind; she had been hoping to get into an argument with the Dark Fae king and make him lose his focus on the safety of the kingdom. But unfortunately for her, Oren remained calm and in denial about the young woman's sudden change in demeanor.

"I'll take my leave. The journal is mine. You don't deserve anything from my father!" Willow yelled. Before Oren could say or do anything, Willow waved her hand, and in a shower of sparks that left behind the scent of dahlias, she was gone.

Alder silently left his hiding spot from within the shadows, no doubt on his way to Nessa's castle just as the now-corrupted Willow was.

Oren sighed and sat down in one of the chairs, then he held his head in his hands. A few moments passed and Nerida walked in, holding Wisp's hand. A look of concern was evident on her face as she saw Oren sitting like he had been utterly defeated.

He glanced at her and sighed. Noticing that perhaps he had something to tell her, she gestured for their daughter to go and play in the courtyard. Once Wisp was out of earshot, Oren told his queen everything.

"Willow says she is with Nessa now. I have no idea what transpired whilst we were all slumbering. I also fear that Adair may not have been the only traitor. Willow stole her father's journal, which contains the layout of this castle. No doubt she intends to hand it over to Nessa." Nerida's hand flew to her mouth in shock at the news. It was unexpected. How could anyone fall for Nessa's lies?

"Where is she now? And if you're talking about Fiore's journal, then did you manage to take it back?" Nerida asked.

Oren's grim expression said it all, but he answered his queen. "Unfortunately, I was unable to get the journal from Willow. If I had, then I would have fought her, and I could not bring myself to harm her."

Nerida was saddened and confused as to why Willow had suddenly changed. The young woman was sweet and selfless from what she knew about her. Outside, the skies became darker, clouds rolling in, once again heralds to the danger that everyone in the court and alliance would be in.

Someone had done something to change Willow, of this the two Dark Fae rulers were certain. Calling Wisp back inside the hall, the Dark Fae queen told her daughter to stay with her father until she made the morning meal, perhaps the last peaceful meal they would have in the days to come.

A figure dressed in red and black made their way toward the entrance of Nessa's castle. The guards did nothing to stop them from entering, instead nodding as they passed through.

The sound of footsteps was heard as the figure walked toward the throne.

"Ah, Willow. You've finally made it. Welcome back to my court."

Nessa's cold voice spoke from where she had been patiently awaiting the young woman's arrival. By Nessa's side, the usually green-eyed Alder with a purple glaze and a blank stare on his face stood motionless.

Black lips formed a smirk as she stood in front of the Dwarf queen. "But of course, Queen Nessa. Once I found out the truth of the matter, I decided to join you."

Nessa chuckled coldly, her plans were coming into fruition and soon the throne and title of high queen would be hers and hers alone. "And what of the layout of Oren's castle? Did you manage to find anything regarding that information?" Nessa inquired.

Willow nodded her head, handing over her father's journal to Nessa. The Dwarf queen couldn't contain her malicious glee at finally having an edge over Oren.

"Excellent work, Willow. You've brought me the very thing I need to destroy the wretched Dark Fae king. Now, I want you to train your powers under King Nash. He seems to have the most knowledge on how your powers work after they have been suppressed for so long. He should be in the sparring hall. If you cannot find it, the guards will point the way," Nessa directed.

Willow nodded her head and turned on her heel. Outside, lightning flashed and thunder roared. A sure sign of a war approaching.

CHAPTER 20

There was a thick tension in the air, the stormy weather once again reflecting the moods of each and every court in the realm.

A war was about to begin. The Dark Fae Court and their allies silently prepared for battle.

Oren sharpened his weapons and gathered his armor, weaving his magic into the metal.

His allies prepared as well, each of them hoping that they wouldn't have to resort to this kind of fighting that hadn't happened in the time since Oren succeeded the throne.

Willow made her way toward the sparring hall, spotting the door and opening it a crack, seeing King Nash fighting his way through the magical obstacle course in a fury of red and silver sparks. Not a moment passed when he noticed the young woman walk into the room, a bored expression on her face. Walking over to her, he stood a head taller than her, cutting an intimidating figure as he narrowed his blood-red eyes.

"You are the secret weapon Nessa was talking about? I can sense that your powers are immense, but you don't have complete control over them. I can teach you to control them, as I'm sure Queen Nessa has told you that I am well versed enough to do so. As long as you follow my orders, then there should be no trouble," he shared.

In Willow's mind, Nessa smirked.

"Tell him that he had better not try and betray me. After all, he wouldn't want his pretty little wife to suffer the consequences of his stupidity now, would he?"

Willow smirked at the Goblin king's speech.

"Oh? Did I hear you correctly, King Nash? You want me to follow your orders? Aside from what Queen Nessa has told me, I have no reasons to trust anyone else. I would think twice if not thrice about taking orders from you. I can easily tell Nessa that you're trying to betray her. After all, whom do you think she really trusts? And I would keep an eye on Hellia. After all, you wouldn't want anything to happen to her. As for my magic lessons, all I need to do is read all the books on magic in the library. So, in essence, I don't need you," she finished with a dark smile, not giving the Goblin king a proper chance to respond, and she walked out of the room, slamming the door behind her.

The Goblin king watched Willow walk away with an air of arrogance. How in the realm did she know of his intentions? He had thought that being under Nessa's control meant that the young woman would be meek and listen to orders without question. However, the Dwarf queen created a bigger problem than she had intended. And the Goblin king could do nothing about that, for if the Dark Fae were to hear these accusations, then she would just use honeyed words to convince Nessa that King Nash was a liar and didn't want to aid her. He couldn't risk the safety of his wife by having any suspicions on him during a time where war was likely about to happen.

So, the Goblin king silently turned and left the room as well, making his way back to the Goblin Court in order to prepare for the war that Nessa so badly wanted to wage with the Dark Fae king.

Willow, having said all that to Nash, had returned to Nessa's throne room. However, upon her arrival, she noticed that the Dwarf queen was not in sight. Sighing in frustration, she asked the guards where the Dwarf queen had gone and when she would return. The guards, not fully realizing the consequences of their actions, laughed coldly in her face and shoved her to the ground.

THUD!

She fell to the ground with such force that the chains on her boots broke off.

"You stupid girl, why would her majesty waste her time with the likes of you?" one of them taunted, and soon, the rest followed like clockwork.

"She's just a weak little girl!" one said.

"I heard her father died in a pool of his own blood, and her mother was hunted down by the previous ruler of the Light Fae Court and killed too! How pathetic!" another sneered.

"Yes, if only her parents were smart enough to accept King Faven's offer!"

Willow felt rage, and then all of a sudden, the crackle of electricity was heard in the air. Red lighting left Willow's fingertips, striking each and every one of the guards who had been taunting her. Screams of agony pierced through the air as the guards fell to the ground, some of them knocked unconscious.

Horrified, the young woman stared down at her hands, feeling sick. Her powers had seemingly acted of their own accord . . . or according to her emotions. Before she could process what had happened, Nessa chose to walk into the room, a wicked smile on her face, a blank-faced Alder trailing behind her.

"Congratulations, Willow. You've achieved the first step in becoming an ally of the Light Alliance. Getting rid of your enemies without hesitation, something I would have done as well. Come, let us prepare for battle with Oren and his allies, no doubt he is preparing things on his side."

Shaking from the impact of what she had just done, the young woman got off the ground and dusted herself off. Nessa laughed coldly, so much so that the throne room may as well have been covered in ice.

The young woman's mind was already a mess, and this shock was only the beginning; Nessa planned to exploit her emotions to make her an unstoppable force of magic in her army.

They walked out and made their way to the armory to make plans on the impending war. Once they arrived, Nessa turned to the young woman, intent on getting more information about Oren so that she could take him down once and for all.

"You must know of his weaknesses, Willow. After all, you were with him for quite some time before coming to your senses," Nessa said.

With a wicked smile on her black-painted lips, Willow turned to Nessa. "Well, Queen Nessa, you know as well as I do that Oren values his family and friends above all else. So, in order to get him to go to war with you, why not send a message?"

Intrigued by Willow's answer, though not comprehending exactly what she meant, the Dwarf queen sported a look of confusion on her face.

Holding back her irritation, Willow expanded for the Dwarf queen. "In order to get Oren, the first person you need to defeat is Prince Lyndell. If you defeat him on the battlefield, you'll be able to defeat the Dark Fae king easily."

Nessa smiled, if one could call the eerie expression on her face that. "It would seem you were very observant of the time you spent with Oren. I am quite glad you came to your senses and joined my side."

The two of them resumed making battle plans with Nessa explaining the layout of the battlefield and the number of weapons and soldiers she had ready to go to war, not to mention her allies. Finishing their planning, Nessa ordered her guards to send messages to each of her allies to meet in the middle of the realm. Once there, they would send a message to Oren. He could either give up his position as the high ruler or else risk going to war with at least half of the realm in the same place where they once used to celebrate living in peace.

Handing Willow a black and gold sword with rubies

embedded in its hilt, the Dwarf queen and Dark Fae left the armory and set off toward the middle of the realm in preparation of a battle.

Silence consumed Oren's castle, the lights casting an eerie glow in the dark halls as clouds concealed the sun, thus no natural light entered through the windows. The Dark Fae king sat on his throne, Nerida by his side amongst the many books and maps that littered the area surrounding them.

Nerida could tell Oren was upset at Willow's betrayal, but as the circumstances were, they couldn't afford to dwell on such thoughts at the moment. The both of them looked at maps, determining the best placement of soldiers based upon their skills. Prior to finding out Willow's betrayal, the Dark Fae king had called a meeting with his allies and informed them of the news.

Anyone could tell that a war was going to happen, so each of his allies made a pledge to aid the Dark Fae king even if it would cost them their lives, though this was something Oren would not let happen.

With a newfound burst of determination despite the grim news, the Dark Fae king would make those who were responsible for the death of his closest friend pay dearly. They would pay even more for turning his friend's daughter against him, for that had been the biggest blow he had been dealt. It had hurt him worse than when he had almost been killed by the moron Heliodor.

Whilst he and Nerida were making plans, Sir Ash came running in, his hair askew and running out of breath, holding a pitch-black envelope, the seal of the Dwarf queen holding it closed.

"Your highness! Nessa has sent a message for you!"

Oren wordlessly took the letter from Sir Ash, breaking the golden seal and reading the contents.

Greetings, your highness,

Though there is really no need for formality at this point, I thought I would do you a favor and humor you. After all, once I become the high queen of this realm, you'll be at my mercy.

I have the daughter of your dearest friend as well as his notes on the layout of your castle. If you surrender now, I'll release the girl and even give you and your family the chance to escape.

—Dwarf Queen Nessa of the Dwarf Court

Clenching the piece of paper in his fist, a look of rage passed on his face.

"How dare she tell me to surrender! The war has barely even started and already she has gathered her alliance in the middle of the realm to try and get me to give up my title! I will gather my army and allies and meet her there. Nessa presumes too much! I will fight to protect my court until my dying breath!"

Turning to Nerida, he gently grasped her hand in his own, placing a kiss on the back.

"My dear, Nerida, I need you to promise me that you will stay and protect Wisp. Should anything happen to me, at least she will have you. Before you protest that you can fight as well, I know. But Wisp needs one of us to be there when she becomes queen of this court. And I don't know of anyone better than you. Promise me."

Nerida wanted more than anything to be able to protect both her king and her daughter. As such, she could only do one thing, and that was to protect Wisp at all costs. With a look of determination and sadness, she nodded.

"I promise, Oren darling. I will keep her safe. I can't make you promise to come back, but please don't let Nessa or Heliodor win. The Dwarf queen's court and her alliance have conspired to take over this court and the realm for far too long," she said.

Oren nodded and stood up, a determined look on his face. "Don't worry, Nerida, I will make them both pay."

Glancing at Sir Ash, he gestured for him to follow as he left the throne room. Nerida watched them both go and stood up as well, getting ready to protect her daughter as the peaceful times in the realm were about to end.

Oren used a spell that left silver and sapphire sparks on his hand to deliver a quick message to his allies, telling them to meet him in the middle of the realm. Promptly after that, the Dark Fae king pulled out his rarely used sword, with a gleaming blue blade, the hilt a shade of the night sky, decorated with tiny star-like gemstones. He also grabbed a pair of silver and blue daggers and tucked them inside of his boots. Placing the sword inside a silver scabbard that hung from his waist, the Dark Fae king fluttered his wings and made his way toward the middle of the realm, hoping to end the madness created by the Light and Dwarf Courts.

Landing on top of a grass-covered hill overlooking the field, Oren took in the surrounding landscape. To his right, a forest bordered the battlefield, and to his left a river flowed with a strong current. Above his head, thick storm clouds continued to roll in as he heard the first clap of thunder in the distance. He spotted Nessa's camp. Golden tents had been set up and the banners of each one of the courts involved with her flowed in the breeze. When he turned to the place where he was supposed to meet with his allies, the Dark Fae king was satisfied to see the same things set up on his side of the battlefield, except the tents were silver in color.

All his allies stood by him, silently awaiting his orders, weapons in hand, eager for the chance to knock down those who dared to look down on them. Looking across the field at Nessa's camp, Oren figured that they were still awaiting his response and thus, were unaware that Oren and his allies had gathered that swiftly. Oren looked at his allies and gave his orders.

"I will take a small group of soldiers with me through the forest to take Willow from Nessa's camp. The rest will follow Prince Lyndell onto the battlefield. They won't expect us to infiltrate their camp from the side on top of the assault from our impenetrable front. We are going to restore peace to this realm!"

Roaring in agreement, Oren's army and his allies charged onto the battlefield, silently at first, but once they reached the center of the field, they cried out as loudly as they possibly could to alert the opposing side.

Meanwhile, Oren and his small group of soldiers hurried into the forest, silently making their way into the enemy camp as rain began to fall. Shouts of surprise from Nessa's soldiers echoed across the field as they began to scramble to assemble their own armies. It was complete and utter chaos. Oren made it to Nessa's camp, sneaking through to find Willow in hopes that bringing her back would undo whatever Nessa had done to her.

Back on the battlefield, swords and other weapons clashed left and right, many creatures pierced and wounded, left lying on the ground. Smoke and ash began to fill the air as some of the tents and banners were set on fire. The Light Alliance was not prepared for an infiltration inside the camp, thus some of the soldiers had been eating and lounging.

Hearing the cries of the soldiers, Willow stepped out from one of the many tents, sword drawn, eyes widening at the chaotic scenes of blood, death, and smoke in the once pristine camp. Gritting her teeth in anger at the idiots that decided to play around instead of keeping watch, she spotted a stray Dark Fae solider sneaking around the tents. She moved to swing at him.

CLANG!

A gleaming blue blade with a black hilt blocked her blow, belonging to none other than Oren.

"Don't you even dare to land a blow on my soldier, Willow! This is not who you are! You need to come to your senses!"

She smirked, further angering the Dark Fae king who did not let that show on his face. Swinging her sword, she aimed to land a blow on Oren, only to be blocked once more.

"I see that you've not gotten over the fact that this is who I am now," Willow spat.

Ignoring her words, the Dark Fae king continued to block her blows, hoping he could tire Willow out and that he could just take her as his prisoner. By this time, the entire camp was aware of the Dark Fae king's presence and the remaining soldiers closed in on his group.

While Oren was distracted, Willow slipped away back into tent where Nessa was. The Dwarf queen, sensing that they were in danger, took Willow and fled back to her castle. Oren stood with his soldiers and fought, as he helplessly watched Nessa escape with Willow in tow.

With many soldiers from both courts losing their lives, the bloody battle continued as magical creatures who were once friends were turned to enemies. They fought to the death, as thunder roared and lightning crashed, much like the soldiers and weapons on the wet battlefield.

ABOUT the AUTHOR

Aiysha Qureshi grew up in the beautiful state of Virginia. Her friends and family are the most important people to her. Inspired by stories her father used to tell her as a child, Aiysha started writing stories of her own, eventually turning it into something she did and still does in her spare time. When she's not writing or spending time with her family, you can find her enjoying a cup of tea with her pet parakeet Oren, named after the main character in her story. Aside from writing, Aiysha also paints, makes jewelry, and takes photographs of nature.